REDEMPTION

REDEMPTION

A MANY LIVES STORY

LAXMI HARIHARAN

THE MANY LIVES UNIVERSE

In a world full of shifters, vampires and immortals, the Many Lives Series begins in present-day Bombay right before a catastrophic natural disaster destroys much of the city. Embark upon a perilous and epic journey as Ruby Iyer and Vikram Roy uncover the secrets of the city—and the demons of their past.

The Many Lives Series is an epic paranormal action-romance series that traces the origin and love stories of one woman's illegitimate descendants—all united by the power of her infamous sword.

ORDER OF READING

Join Laxmi's newsletter to get her
starter library free here:
http://smarturl.it/Laxmi

THE STORY SO FAR...

In 2014, Ruby Iyer harnessed the power of an ancient sword. She triggered killer storms that wiped out Bombay, among other cities.

By 2060, Bombay rebuilt itself to become the shining hope of the East.

Meanwhile economic depression has forced many to migrate towards this beacon of prosperity.

Shifters and humans once at odds, now co-exist in Bombay. Both united by their hatred for the rules that the Council of Bombay imposes on citizens.

The Council's goal: economic progress.

Bombay has also attracted vampires. Lethal, powerful creatures led by the scientist Daniel Winter.

Daniel wants Ruby's sword so he can harness the forces of nature to do his bidding.

The same sword that Ruby's descendent, Leana Iyeroy has in her possession.

Leana is the first wolf-shifter in Ruby's bloodline.

Mikhail is the first of the Ascendants: a group of immortals whose mission is to help humans defeat evil.

Redemption is Leana and Mikhail's story.

REDEMPTION

When differences tear fated mates apart

LEANA

I submit to no one—not even him. Not till I was taken.
A terrible emptiness now tears me apart. For,
he's just…gone
Cast adrift, I'm alone. So alone, in the dark
Will I *see* him again?

MIKHAIL

I never needed anyone
Then I met her, a cage fighter, my shifter. Mine.
The one I must protect
Through many lives I've searched for her
Now I more than need her—I want her. In my life, in my blood.
Her, only her.

Reclusive designer Mikhail Anton blames wolf-shifters for his memory loss, refusing to accept the signs that he is immortal. On meeting Leana Iyeroy, a female cage-fighter and shifter, Mikhail is drawn to her in ways he can't identify.

When vampires threaten Leana, Mikhail must acknowledge his abilities to rescue her from certain death. Can Leana and Mikhail team up to save each other, before their differences destroy everything they love

CHAPTER 1

Bombay, Ubud Island, June 2061

THE MALE SHIFTER SNARLS AT me across the fighting cage. Is he wolf? Man?

He's both.

He's neither.

He's like me.

We, the hybrids who don't belong anywhere, end up here. On the island where it all started.

Forty-seven years ago, my grandma Ruby touched her sword to the altar of the temple that stands in a corner of this arena. She unleashed the tsunamis that swept away much of the old world, including Bombay. The city has since been rebuilt.

Now we fight here every fortnight.

We come here to kill.

"Kill!" The hybrid roars and, pushing away from the bars, leaps. He comes straight at me. My brain stutters with fear, hands gripping my sword. *Ruby's sword.*

Then, my reflexes kick in, and I slide aside. Just. In. Time.

The hybrid crashes right next to me, and the heavy axe he wields goes flying. He falls close enough for his body heat to brush against me. Close enough even for my skin to shrivel with disgust.

My heart rams against my ribs, sending the blood thundering

in my temples. My senses open. I look at my opponent, 'see' him. Dirty red and orange from the hybrid blaze out. The colors slam into me with the force of a physical punch.

I gasp. Squeeze my eyes shut and close down my senses. Shoving the creature out of my psychic space, I discard that peek into his soul. Shut him out.

Silence.

Before I can raise my sword, the shifter is back on his feet. Bending low, he kicks my legs out from under me.

I fall on my back, losing my weapon. My head hits the ground, shooting white sparks behind my eyes. I lay there stunned as the shifter reaches for his axe.

I want to get up, but I can't. Don't move. The voice over the loudspeaker begins the countdown to death:

"One."

Pain cuts through me, making me gasp.

"Two."

My gut churns.

"Three."

The bile rises to my throat.

"Four."

The axe lowers.

"Five."

I will not shut my eyes, will face death head on.

"Six."

Take a deep breath.

"Seven."

In.

"Eight."

Out.

A pair of shoulders blocks out the harsh overhead light.

"Nine."

It's him.

Teo? Is that you, Teo?

No, it can't be.

I killed Matteo: He's better dead than his essence being taken by a vampire. I know that. Yet, I'll never forgive myself for it. Now I pay for my sins by cage-fighting. Teasing death; taunting it.

Now it's here.

The hybrid is thrust aside with such force that his body arcs through the air.

What the—?

I'm pulled to my feet. My gaze clashes with his, and holds.

Silver-green eyes.

Like ice-chips on a frozen sea. Calm. *Unlike me.* Me, whose emotions are too near the surface.

A roar of pain makes me start. I peer around the stranger, at the fallen hybrid. Whoever this guy is, he'd been strong enough to throw the beast. He bought me time to recover.

How did he even enter the cage?

"Get back in the game! Use your sword," he snaps, this man who's come from nowhere.

No, he's not a man. He doesn't smell fragrant, like a human. Doesn't smell like dense vegetation, like hybrid-shifters. None of that sickly sweet smell of vampires, either.

He smells like…like fresh snow and something else deeper, darker, more intense. Like wood-smoke on a warm afternoon.

What species is he? I wonder. But can't bring myself to ask.

Instead, "Let me die," I blurt out.

I failed to protect Teo. *I deserve to die.*

Tears prick my eyes, but I don't wipe them away.

3

Then, he slaps me, and all thoughts escape. Anger flares: a violet spark that tries to ignite. The wolf pounds against the walls I've thrown around it, pushing me to transform.

Whatever you do Leana, don't shift. My father Luke's voice stops me.

The spark inside me dies. I'm taken back to a different fight, when we faced off against a vampire. Luke had warned me then not to reveal my wolf form. If I did, the vampire would know I was Ruby's bloodline. He'd take me and the sword, Luke had said. But I couldn't stop myself. I shifted. Luke had tried to save me from the vampire and been killed.

I blame my wolf for my father's death. I haven't been able to shift since. Instead, the animal's pent-up rage fuels my fights.

"Fight," the male growls.

I focus on his voice, *his eyes.*

Those cold-fire eyes burn through my thoughts, clearing my head.

He nods. Stepping aside as I telescope in on the hybrid.

Before the hybrid can recover, I move. Seize my sword and leap. Almost blind with rage, adrenaline pumping, I bring the sword down on his head. On his ugly head. The hybrid jerks up with a roar, flinging me aside.

I land on my side, screaming as pain jars through me, only to spring right up.

The shifter too is on his feet. Teeth bared, he moves toward me. But I am already there. Muscles tense, leaning forward, sword outstretched. I let the wolf inside brush up against my skin. Feel its energy course through me.

Become me.

I slash down and the blade goes through his forehead. When I yank out the sword, blood sprays over me.

The hybrid crashes. The impact of the body vibrates through the ground. The force of it catches me unawares, and I fall, too.

Next to him.

Silence.

Then, one of us moves. And it's not him.

CHAPTER 2

I STUMBLE TO MY FEET, still gripping the sword. My opponent's face is a bloodied mess.

He's dead.

The wolf inside bares its teeth in victory, then pushes against my skin. Asks for more. It always wants more. More violence, more blood.

But not today.

Enough for today.

I clamp down on the wolf and fling it back into the cage inside, slamming the door after it. To my relief, it obeys. Stays inside. *This time.*

The adrenaline ebbs, and pain crashes through me in a wave that has my knees shaking. Sweat drips into my eyes.

I stay paralyzed, not believing I'm still alive.

I don't hear the crowds throw themselves against the cage, screaming my name.

Barely notice when the referee raises my arm. "Leana, this female shifter, is the winner of today's fight," he declares.

The crowds surge, yelling in disbelief.

No one cares that a stranger intruded and helped me win the fight.

There are no rules in these fights. A stark contrast to how the Council runs the city outside.

The commentator's voice pours over the speakers: "What a surprise upset. Leana faces the ultimate challenge in a fortnight. On the day of the blood moon, she takes on a bloodier"—He cackles at his own joke—"opponent. But will she make it through?"

A fresh burst of pain cuts through my side. Biting my lips, I stop myself from groaning. I want no weakness captured by the camera trained on me.

These fights air on the sole underground virtual network in the city. Personal communication devices are at a premium since the tsunamis wiped out rare earth metal reserves. But these fights are so popular that almost every shifter and human will tune in at secret viewing points.

Sliding my arm out of the referee's grasp, I stagger away.

I should be grateful I'm alive.

I made it thanks to the male with silver-green eyes. It's only then I realize he's disappeared. Gone, as he'd come.

Silent, like he isn't of this world.

But he was real, all right.

I'd felt his touch on my shoulders, seen those eyes. And I had sensed him. In those few seconds, that silver-green essence of his had bled into me, into my skin. It had shocked me, pushed me to live.

Pushed me so I had almost dropped the barriers, almost let out the wolf. The animal inside me had trusted him, too. In those few seconds, my wolf had known the stranger wouldn't hurt me.

The only other time the wolf had been this certain was with Teo. My wolf loved Teo. Saw Teo as a safe harbor.

This time as I think of Teo, the pain that normally cripples me is gone, replaced instead with a softer regret.

I don't know why, but walking away from the fight, I feel

lighter than I have in a long time.

I reach the human waiting to hand over the credits I've won and push all thoughts of the stranger out of my mind.

Paper has long since become a rarity and now my fingers clench the chips that can be bartered for services in this new world. These credits should keep the kids at the orphanage going for the next six months. It'll even pay the rent on my tattoo studio.

Shrugging off my torn shirt, I use it to wipe the blood off the sword. Making sure to remove any stains from the pattern on the scabbard. My fingers trace the grooves. *What does this symbol mean?*

Sliding the sword into the scabbard, I heave it over my vest, across my back. Ensuring the strap is secure, I walk toward the exit.

No longer a warrior-shifter, all I am now is a wounded female: scrawny, clad in leather pants and a torn vest.

A prickle at the nape of my neck. The sensation of being watched has me swinging around. My eyes scan the sea of faces: shifters, vampires, and some species I don't even recognize. *But not him.* I don't see him.

I'd only had a glimpse of this male who saved my life in the ring, but I know I'd pick him out anywhere. Then the sensation fades, and I know he's gone.

Weariness rushes over me. I feel empty, and for that I am grateful. I may tell myself I am fighting for the credits, or that I have a death wish, but really *this* is the reason. I battle to purge myself of all emotions.

Little do I know it's a taste of what is to come.

CHAPTER 3

Sometimes you see a person and you know it's meant to be. Yet, you fight that feeling. Till what is simple becomes twisted.

Mikhail looks at the female shifter as she passes by him. She's so close that if he put out his hand, he could touch her cheek.

Leana.

Her name. He knows *that* much, from the announcement earlier.

Mikhail watches as the female adjusts the strap of the scabbard between her breasts, and his eyes fall on the rise-fall-rise of her chest. His gaze travels over the swell of the vest that stretches tight across, outlining her nipples. Even though she doesn't even notice him, and despite being surrounded by jostling crowds, Mikhail finds himself aroused.

Heat twists his gut with such suddenness that he gasps.

It's the second time he's surprised himself in the space of an hour. The first was when he'd seen Leana fall to the ground in the cage… and not move.

She'd lain so still he'd been sure she'd been hurt badly or worse—that she'd been killed. Before he could stop himself, he ran through the crowd, breaking through to the front.

He overcame the guard at the cage entrance, unlocked the gate, and ran toward Leana, all in a matter of seconds.

As he leaned over her, she moaned and he relaxed a little.

Alive! She was alive.

Then, her eyes snapped open and locked onto his. Those amber eyes gleaming gold. She stared not-blinking, and tilted her head in a gesture so *not* human that he sensed... felt the wolf inside her come alert.

She reached out to him with her inner self, with her very soul. He felt her brush up against him, as she sensed his essence.

For the first time since he woke on that beach with no memory of how he got there, Mikhail came alive.

All these years he'd been only half-awake. Been living a lie. And now that she was here, he'd snapped completely into his body.

And even as he denies the thought, something in him insists she is it. When he'd seen her, he'd also seen right through to the pattern that was her. For that is how Mikhail understands the world. Through patterns in numbers, in music...in people, too.

And in Leana, he saw the graceful symphony of her soul: a delicate strength, a lust for life, to survive.

It all became clear to him then.

She was the reason he had been allowed to live. The reason he'd been swept up to the shores of *this* city. It had to be here, now. *Now* is when everything is right, in this arena, surrounded by those thirsting for her blood.

Now is the right time for him to have met her.

It all feels so right it makes him wary, for Mikhail is not given to impulses.

The only reason he's at the cages tonight is to study the shifters for weaknesses. He'll use the findings to design the Hive Net. A psychic construct that will allow the Council of Bombay to connect every shifter to one virtual network. A powerful psychic weapon enabling the Council to track the minds of every single shifter in the city.

It's the biggest project of his life. One from which he is going to make enough money to last him a long time.

It hadn't crossed his mind that what he's doing is wrong. That he's helping the Council subjugate an entire species. Why should it? When all these years he's been suspicious of shifters.

Nineteen years ago, he washed up on the shores of Bombay with no memory of who he was. Yet, the one thing he's always known is that he doesn't trust shifters.

But then he looked into Leana's eyes, realized that she filled a gap in him. One he didn't even know existed.

He also sensed the wolf in her, and realized she couldn't shift. That she was trapped in this body, this city... *Like him.*

Now as she walks away from him, a part of him insists that whatever he feels for her is not true. This emotion she evokes in him is but lust. All he has to do is find her and sate his need. And that should be that.

Mikhail has no idea how wrong he is.

CHAPTER 4

A week later

I STEP OVER THE LOW wall separating the orphanage from the beach. My still-healing wound from the fight twinges. I wince in pain, then walk across the small garden leading to the main building.

Following the tsunamis, successive downturns had crashed the economies of many Western cities; but the newly rebuilt Bombay had thrived in the new world. Migrants had arrived seeking a new life here, in this shining hope of the East. And been housed in a refugee camp nicknamed the Jungle.

Shifters had once attacked the Jungle in the hope of getting the attention of the Council. Now they had their own space— Shifter Town. Once that happened, the fighting too stopped.

Humans and shifters are now united against a common enemy: the city Council.

The Ganesh Interfaith Orphanage is between Shifter Town and the Jungle.

As I walk through the playground, little Yasmin waves to me from the swings. She shrieks in delight when her friend pushes her up into the air. Her features glow, eyes closed in rapture.

Simple pleasures I never had, growing up.

My pack-guardian had insisted on moving place to place, fearful the Council would track us down. She'd cared for me since Maya, my blood mother, died. She was killed by her brother, Jai, the then-Guardian of Bombay.

My birth father, Luke, survived. Grief-stricken on losing Maya, he'd gone missing, only to surface when I turned eighteen. To avenge my mother, Luke had killed Jai and taken his sword.

He'd found me and given it to me. He said it was my legacy. That the sword belonged to Maya. And to her mother, Ruby, before that. Now it was mine.

But I didn't want it.

I came to Bombay to return it to Jai's son, Rohan. Instead, I used the sword to kill Matteo, after the vamps turned him.

Now I use the sword to protect myself, and the orphans.

"Leana!" Rohan walks toward me. Dark shoulder length hair, frames his chiseled features. A sleeveless T-shirt shows off his biceps, faded jeans tight around his hips. Rohan always tries to be macho. Perhaps he tries too hard.

As he comes close, his face breaks into a grin. A surge of affection runs through me. Throwing his arm around me, Rohan lifts me off the ground.

His scent, a whiff of dried earth mixed with the tang of sea air, is confusing. It's almost comforting, and yet not.

There's something disconcerting about Rohan. He's family, but never feels like it to me.

His muscles tense as he holds up my weight. He grips my waist, squeezing it, hurting me. I struggle until he lowers me. He slides me all the way down the length of his body; a part of me starts in surprise.

He wants to draw comfort from my body.

Yeah, that's all it is.

Indigo eyes stare at me. Eyes filled with secrets. It's like look-ing at myself, except not.

He's a more intense version of me.

Twisted.

Rohan had found me thru Aki, here in this orphanage.

He, the son of the Mayor of the city.

Me, a runway half-breed.

Both united by our hate for our families. Except, I'm an orphan. Rohan prefers to act like he's one.

Another scream of delight from the girls cuts through my thoughts, and I struggle out of his grasp. To my relief, he lets me go. I don't want to upset him. After all, he's all the family I have left. Besides, I do like him.

Though not the way he wants.

"I'm here to meet Aki," I say, hoping to be on my way.

When he stays quiet, I find myself speaking to fill the silence. To stop him from staring at me.

"I wanted to give him this," I say.

Dipping my hand into my jeans pocket, I pull out the credit chips from the cage fight. He holds his palm out. When I move to drop the chips in, he raises his hand, gripping mine, crushing the chips to my skin.

"Aki's gone to meet the Council," his eyes widen.

I try to pull my hand from his grasp but he doesn't let go.

Closing the gap between us, he towers over me.

I tilt my head back to look at him, and flinch at the unspoken plea in his eyes. Eyes that devour me.

He wants me.

He's never been this open about what he desires from me.

"The Council?"

I tug my hand and when he lets go, I take a step back. Try to slide away from him but he follows, closing the gap between us.

I stiffen, a coil of panic fluttering in my belly.

I know I can protect myself. I'm stronger than him. Yet, the intent in his actions takes me by surprise. Discomfort curls around me.

"Aki's gone to discuss a possible coalition. He wants to unite humans and shifters against the vampires."

Rohan's voice is careless, but his casualness gives him away.

He knows more than he's letting on.

"What do you know about the vamps?" I ask.

A guilty look crosses Rohan's face, gone so quickly I might have imagined it.

"I don't want to be the one facing them," he says. "Unless, of course, you have a weapon powerful enough to kill even vamps." His eyes go to the sword on my back. "But you can kill them with *that*, can't you, Leana?"

I start.

It still hurts to be reminded of killing Matteo. Why is Rohan being this unkind? A prickle of wariness runs up my spine. I push it away.

This is my cousin. He won't do anything to harm me.
Will he?

"When did you realize this was Jai's sword?" I ask.

I never bothered to hide the sword from Rohan, sure he recognized it, too. But in the time we've known each other, he's never asked about it. Not till now.

I never wanted to be the keeper of the sword, never wanted access to the power it imparts to Ruby's descendants: those like me who share the lineage of Catherine of Braganza.

Not waiting for his reply, I slide out the sword and offer it to my cousin.

"I am tired of the bloodshed this sword brings with it," I say. "We can put an end to it right now. Take it." I push the sword toward him.

He looks at the blade, then at me.

He doesn't react, though.

He recognized this sword from the moment he saw me with it. I'd been sure he'd ask for it, ask how I got it, but he hadn't.

Now as he looks at me, his eyes steady, I realize he knows. He knows my father killed his to get the sword.

Taking a step forward, he grips my hand curled around the hilt.

"You'd give it to me, even knowing the next blood moon is only a week away?" he asks. "Only the second blood moon since 2014."

Legends say on the night of the blood moon, a direct descendant of Catherine of Braganza can use the sword to invoke the forces of nature—and harness the force to do their bidding.

During the 2014 blood moon, Ruby used the sword to trigger the tsunami that destroyed Bombay.

Twenty-five years later, Maya, my mother, had done the same. But Jai, Rohan's father, stopped Maya. He killed her.

Thinking about the bloodshed in my family makes me feel faint.

Ruby's blood runs through both me and Rohan. *Both of us can harness the power of the sword.*

Now the next blood moon is upon us, and this time *I* have the sword.

Both Ruby and Maya had used the sword and paid for it. Ruby had brought about the destruction of Bombay, and Maya had been killed. I am determined not to be next.

"Take it," I say again. "It's yours. Use it as you must."

It occurs to me that Luke had told me something similar, too. That when the time was right, I'll know what to do with the sword.

Perhaps this is what he meant? For, if Luke hadn't taken it, the sword would have passed onto Rohan.

Rohan pulls the sword, and me, toward him. I am sure he's going to take the sword. Instead, he says, "I've never wanted the sword. It's you I want, Leana. Only you."

His eyes hold mine, drawing me to look into their depths. I recoil at the obsessive glint there. But a part of me is fascinated, too. This man knows how forbidden any relationship between us is, yet he never stopped pursuing me.

Still, I never thought he'd give up his claim on the sword for me. *That* surprises me.

Does he want me that much?

He steps closer, his chest grazing my nipples. I cringe and try to move away, but his grip stays firm, doesn't let go. The sword remains between us. The warmth from his body slams into me, a contrast to the cold scabbard digging into my skin. I sense his desperation. That madness I'd ignored so far.

Rohan won't stop.

He'll do anything to get to me, even hurt me. *And if he can't have me, he won't let anyone else, either.*

"I told you I'd wait for you, but my patience is wearing thin, Leana," he says.

My insides churn with fear. *Does he already know my heart is pulled toward another?* Toward a stranger with silver-green eyes.

Rohan's been there for me through the past few months. He helped me through the difficult days after Teo's death. He'd been more than patient. He promised he'd be my friend, and had stayed true to that.

But now he knows: friendship is all I can ever offer. And for him, that's not enough.

His face descends toward me, his eyes pleading. I want to run from him, but I can't. My legs won't move. I feel trapped.

Yasmin appears next to me and tugs my shirt. "We're going to the beach to play," she says.

Her eyes dart from Rohan to me. She must feel the tension between us.

"Come." She pulls at me.

Rohan lets me go so suddenly I stumble. I'd have fallen but Yasmin holds me firm, almost dragging me now in her hurry to get to the beach.

The breath whooshes out of me.

"Leana."

Rohan's voice stops me. I grip Yasmin's hand tighter. When she winces, I loosen my fingers. But don't let go of her.

I don't turn, either.

He walks up to me, stops right behind me, so close that I feel the heat from his body reach out toward me. But this time, I move out of the way. This time, I will not be weak.

Dropping the little girl's hand, I touch her cheek. Gesturing to the beach I say, "Go, I'll join you in a second."

When she runs off, I face him, arms on my hips, stance aggressive.

"What?" I snap, letting the impatience show through.

His jaw hardens. His lower lip thrusts out, giving him an obstinate look. He's persistent, my cousin.

"You know I can't let you go, Leah," he says, his voice stiff. "I'll have you one way or the other."

I wince when he uses my nickname. Coming from him, it sounds almost obscene. I know he does it purposely to emphasize that we are bound by blood.

"You can't force me to feel something I don't," I say, my

voice flat, final.

His eyes grow darker, turning almost black.

"We'll see, shall we?" he says.

The hint of menace in his voice makes me blink in surprise. I've hurt his ego, angered him more than I thought possible.

A mistake.

I should've known he isn't going to let go of me, not that easily.

Much later, his words will come back to haunt me.

Rohan never did like to lose.

CHAPTER 5

Two days later

MIKHAIL IS THROBBING, AND IT'S not just from pain. He rams his fist into the speed-bag, furious the female shifter from the cages is still in his thoughts. Even now when he closes his eyes, he can see her fall, can taste the fear that knifed through him.

Blind panic had him jumping into the ring, and he almost gave himself away that day.

He'd almost revealed that he is stronger than shifters and humans, that he has abilities he still doesn't fully understand. *That he's not human.*

Nineteen years ago, he'd dragged his shattered body off the beach, collapsed on the porch of this very bungalow, the one he now owned. He'd woken up with no memories of his life before that day.

He's no closer to finding out what he is. The loneliness a constant ache he carries around inside.

It's one reason he prefers to keep a low profile. He has no friends, not unless you count coders in the underbelly of the city.

Or perhaps he prefers not to be social. For Mikhail has no past to speak of. All he has are fleeting images and pictures that never stay long enough…Except for those eyes. Indigo eyes that stared down at him.

Eyes that saw through to his soul.

Then, they were shut out. The water had closed in, covering those eyes.

Closing over him.

And when he saw Leana collapse, that same feeling swept over him. Of falling, falling and losing the one thing that was most important.

He knew then she was the one he'd been searching for all these years. Except Leana's eyes are amber, not indigo.

Yet, he looked into them and saw his own soul.

A chill runs down his back.

He swears aloud and punches the bag so hard it flies off the hook. Crashes with a loud thump.

Silence.

"Fifth one this month."

A reluctant smile tugs Mikhail's lips.

"Don't you have anything better to do but keep track of my sins, old man?" Mikhail asks.

There's an exasperated sigh as Devein, his housekeeper, walks into the room.

"You do a good enough job of it yourself," he says.

Mikhail barks out a laugh. Picking up a towel, he wipes the sweat running down his face. His gaze falls on a violin in the corner of the room. It peeks out from a half-opened case. He can't remember the last time he played it. Once he enjoyed music for its purity. Its simplicity. Then, he got caught up in the race to make money.

Shoving away the guilt, he walks to the table at the end of the room. The towel slips from his hand, forgotten as he stares at the hologram floating above a sleek tablet.

As he looks into the blueprint in the hologram, everything else fades. He lets the music of the design hums through him.

He no longer sees the clutter in the room, or hears the sound of the waves in the distance.

All he feels is the purity of the design. Geometric forms: circles flush with feminine energy intersected with angular lines.

Mikhail waits for the calmness to wash over him, for the pattern to draw him in, drown him in its purity...*Leana's face,* fear twisting her features, as she faced off the male shifter, flashes in front of his eyes. Mikhail jerks, his focus interrupted.

And *that* is unusual.

He knows then, there is no putting it off. He has to bed the female shifter, get her out of his system.

"Are you going to send the design to the Council?" Devein interrupts his thoughts. "With the money you made, you don't need to design for them anymore, you know?"

Devein is right. And yet, creating psychic design is the only thing Mikhail's good at. Patterns that seem mysterious, and yet always gave up their secrets. Unlike his own past—the biggest secret of them all.

"Sometimes I regret getting you that design project with the Council," Devein adds. "You spend too long staring at that screen. It's not healthy, Mikhail."

It was Devein's connections that led to Mikhail's first assignment with the Council. He had continued to be the liaison between them. The Council only knew that Devein had access to a brilliant designer. But they didn't know who it was: the only way to ensure Mikhail's safety.

"Worried about me, old man?" Mikhail asks, feeling a rush of affection for his friend.

Devein's the *only* person in the world Mikhail cares for.

Except for the shifter with amber eyes.

Devein chuckles. A smile lights up his face, softening his

features and for a second, he's the same Devein from twenty years ago.

Only older.

Mikhail looks closer to the twenty-four years he'd been when they first met. For he ages at one-fourth the speed that humans do.

"So, you've met someone...?" Devein's voice trails off, the lingering traces of a grin on his face.

Mikhail stiffens, taken aback. Is he that easy to read?

"Don't look so surprised," Devein says, his voice only half-joking. "You do need other living beings to survive, you know?"

"Right!" Mikhail dismisses his friend's words with a laugh.

He looks at the design again. The best damn one he's ever created.

So good, he must get it etched on his skin. It's a little ritual of his, to tattoo the best patterns on himself. The feel of the needle breaking his skin, those ripples of pain tearing through him, grounding him, makes him feel...human.

And Leana runs a tattoo studio in Shifter Town. His network of coders had tracked her down in no time.

Switching off the sleek tablet, so the hovering design disappears, he tosses the device over to Devein who catches it.

"You forget how privileged you are sometimes." Devein frowns.

Thanks to his work for the Council, Mikhail has access to communication devices, something very few did. But he knows Devein's comment is not about that.

"What are you implying?" he asks.

Devein hesitates. "All I am saying is that you should be more grateful for your exceptional abilities. Yet you insist on using it only to make money."

"What's wrong with that?" Mikhail demands. "When I arrived here, you were the only one who cared. Not humans and not the shifters, weak and emotional as both these species are. Besides, I hate shifters."

And yet he'd been attracted to Leana – a shifter.

Mikhail pushes that thought away, too.

"I know you are convinced the shifters beat you up and threw you into the sea, but if it hadn't been for that, you wouldn't have discovered your psychic abilities too," Devein says, his voice soft.

Mikhail hesitates, knowing this much is true.

His ability to handle a gun, and the hand-to-hand combat skills he'd woken up with, had convinced him he'd been some kind of a soldier in that life he doesn't remember.

But that's all in the past.

He puts up his hand, stopping Devein when the other man would've spoken more.

"Take the design to the Council," Mikhail says, already walking away.

"Mikhail." Devein's voice stops him. "By giving the Council the blueprint for the Hive Net, you are helping them initiate a collective consciousness. One that will allow them to track and suppress shifters. You are destroying the balance between the species, leaving this city wide open for the vampires to take control."

When Mikhail doesn't answer, Devein continues, "If the Council uses your program, you will be responsible for the vampires destroying this city."

Mikhail knows Devein is right.

Still, his job is to design for the Council and get the money from them. That's where his responsibility ended.

Did it?

For the first time doubt crosses his mind. Then, pushing it aside, he picks up his jacket.

In minutes, he's on his bike and gunning it down the street, driven by one thing: to see that female shifter again.

Little does he know that when he returns, everything in his life will have changed.

CHAPTER 6

An hour later

AFTER PARKING HIS BIKE OUTSIDE Leana's tattoo studio in Shifter Town, Mikhail walks up the short driveway. He enters the little building and finding no one in the reception area, walks into the main studio space inside. His feet crunch on tattoo needles strewn on the floor. An overturned chair lies to the side, and there's ink splashed on the walls.

A groan makes him start.

Rushing across the studio, Mikhail bursts into the adjoining room and freezes.

A large male with broad shoulders holds Leana by her neck. Her legs dangle off the floor. Before Mikhail can react, the giant throws Leana against the wall.

She slams against the hard surface. Her sword clatters to the floor, and she goes down.

"No!"

Yelling at the brute to stop, Mikhail runs toward him, only to come to a standstill halfway.

Leana's already on her feet and sprinting toward her tormentor.

Her movements so fast they blur; she springs at him from across the distance, slamming into him.

The male topples backward, Leana atop him.

Her thighs grip his neck, squeezing it. She holds up her arms, palms gripped together.

She slams it down against his nose. The sound of bone breaking is audible across the distance and then, blood spurts out.

Grabbing the large male's hair, Leana jerks his head up, only to ram it down.

Another audible crack as the surface fractures; the split through the tiles runs toward Mikhail, then past him. Behind Mikhail, something falls over from the impact. But he doesn't hear it.

Mikhail is riveted by the look on Leana's face.

Lips drawn back in a snarl, her eyes narrow with focus: the gold in them glistening, glowing amber. Her very being is concentrated in those eyes. Eyes that look at the brute with such hatred that the force of her feelings hit Mikhail across that space.

Mikhail has never felt this intensity on anyone before.

Leana once again rams her fists down.

A howl erupts from the brute, and black liquid spews out from his forehead.

He thrashes, throwing Leana to the side. She hits the ground, lies there winded.

And then the brute is on his feet, baring his lips. Fangs dropping at the sides of his jaws, he prepares to leap on her.

Mikhail hears someone screaming and knows it's him. He's screaming to her to save herself. And he's afraid. So afraid.

All thoughts of why he came here in the first place—to have his way with her—goes out of his head.

All he knows is this blinding fear that he'll lose her. Again. And Mikhail knows he can't.

He'd loved her that first time too and had lost her then, and this time he can't let her go. Images pour over him, transporting him back to that ship. To those dreams that haunt him at night: indigo eyes staring at him, tear-filled eyes that call out for help.

Then Leana screams, the sound punching through the images in his head.

It propels him into action. He leaps forward at the same time the vampire launches himself at Leana. But he's there first. Mikhail shoves his body between Leana and the creature.

The smell of dry ice, ozone, and something sweet like rotting fruit, fills Mikhail's nostrils. The vamp slams into him. But Mikhail doesn't give way.

Gripping the vampire by its throat, he heaves it up, muscles straining, and flings it away. Slams it back, all the way back, against the wall. The vampire goes right through it, before hitting the ground outside the studio.

It lies stunned, before stumbling to its feet.

Once more, Mikhail moves. One leap takes him over the broken wall. He lands next to the vamp.

In one fluid moment, Mikhail has the vampire by its neck. Raising it up, he tries to twist it. The sweat pouring down his hands makes him lose his grip, and the body falls to the ground.

He looks up in time to see Leana follow him over the broken wall. She lands next to him, sword in hand. Her breath coming in short bursts.

He looks from her to the vampire, only to find its limbs still moving.

Mikhail curses aloud, but before he can do anything, Leana raises her sword. She brings it down, severing the vampire's neck with one clean swipe.

Purple and brown fluid bubbles out. The stench of copper and pungent sewage washes over them, making them both step back.

Leana coughs, burying her nose in the crook of her arm.

Mikhail hauls her away from the dead vampire, and back into the studio.

They stand there, looking at each other.

She's still, predator still. A low growl bubbles up from her throat.

He puts up his hands, palms up, his gesture meant to calm. She goes quiet. Those golden eyes are wary, the flames in them so alive he can't stop staring.

A dense wave of power rushes out from her, reaching out to him across the distance. It slams him in the chest and his breath catches.

A coil of desire tightens his belly, taking him by surprise, and he swears aloud. The sound of his own voice refocuses his mind.

It also makes her look at him closely. He knows the exact moment when she recognizes him from the cages, for a wary look comes into her eyes.

The gold in them deepens further, darkening to hard points of burnt amber.

"You?" she exclaims. "What are you doing here?"

He slants his head, his eyes flashing to the broken wall, through which the body of the fallen vampire is still visible.

When he looks back at her, it is to see her jaw harden. She offers a grudging, "Thanks."

"I saved your life," he says. "You owe me more than just a thanks."

His voice shivers over her skin, the edges clipped with the thread of an accent she can't quite place. He doesn't sound local. Yet, wherever he's from he's been in this city long enough for the sounds of Bombay to seep into his words.

She looks at him unblinking. A trickle of sweat, rolls down

her brow. Down her neck. To the thin T-shirt stretched across her chest.

His eyes follow it. Sliding down to her jutting nipples, slipping over the concave dent of her stomach. Lower still to the apex of her thighs, and feels his throat go dry.

He takes his time about it.

When he meets her gaze again, her cheeks are flushed, and she's breathing fast.

She's as aroused as him.

Leana walks to a small table. Picking up a scabbard, she slides her sword into it, before shrugging it over her back.

Then she turns.

On her face, a look he can't quite place. Her amber eyes glint with intent. Closing the distance between them, she pulls his face down and captures his lips.

Her touch goes right to his core. Her scent: sandalwood and jasmine, sinks into him. The heat from her skin—a furnace.

He can feel those emotions vibrating inside her. Tightly coiled and yet so close to the surface. It excites him and for a second, he loses control. Forgets where he is, that the remains of a vampire lay not far from them.

There is only her.

Burying his fingers in her hair, he hauls her close and deepens the kiss. When he thrusts his tongue into her mouth, her taste pours through him. Liquid desire. He shudders. Feels an answering shiver from her.

Then she grips his forearms and squeezes with enough pressure that he lets go.

When she steps back, he shudders again: this time, with the pain of being separated from her. And that confuses him even more.

He's never had this reaction to anyone before. Not to a human. *Never to a shifter.* It's the last thing he expected to feel: this lust for a hybrid, for a species he doesn't care for. It doesn't fit the pattern he's drawn up for his life.

Air rushes between them, slicing through the lingering heat.

"Will that do?" she asks, her voice firm.

About to respond, something makes him pause. A ticking sound that kicks in from the other room.

Even as her eyes widen, Mikhail grabs her hand. He pulls her along so fast, she stumbles.

But he doesn't stop.

Drags her with him, and keeps going.

Run, get her to safety.

They are out of the door of the studio, up the short driveway. Half-way to the road, a massive boom sounds out behind them. Then, rubble rains down: cement, tiles, stones.

Mikhail throws her down, covering her body with his.

As the dust flows over them, he wonders why the vampires want to hurt her.

CHAPTER 7

ADRENALINE POURS INTO MY BLOODSTREAM as my heart races. Around us, the remnants of what was once my studio pour over us. His body pushes mine into the ground, and I can barely breathe.

My breasts are crushed against the hard planes of his chest. His thighs grip mine. I'm surrounded by him. That fresh snow and wood-smoke smell of his zings through me.

When the sounds of falling debris finally subside, he raises himself on his forearms. Dust covers his hair, turning his face grey, so his eyes shine down at me. The silver-green glints like moonlight lit from behind. *Cold fire that will not leave me unmarked.*

A dense plume of heat spools off him, surrounding me, tugging at my lower belly. We've both escaped certain death, and perhaps that makes me even more conscious that I'm alive. I'm here with the most intriguing male I have met in my life.

My tongue flicks out to touch my dry lips. His eyes follow the gesture and when they meet mine, they are colorless pools of light, so clear I see myself in them.

He wants me. He's wanted me from the moment he jumped into the cage to rescue me.

This is the second time he's risked his life for me.

I want to ask him why he did it, but I can't. Can't take my eyes of the pulse thudding at his temple. It echoes my heart.

He lowers his face, nose almost touching mine. Warm breath sears my cheek.

"You okay?" he whispers, voice husky.

The sound scrapes against my already sensitive nerve endings, and I wince as liquid heat pours through my veins.

I nod even as my eyes flutter down.

As I wait.

Wait.

Wait, for him to kiss me.

Then, a rush of air hits me as he moves away.

When I open my eyes, he's standing over me. His features are closed. Did I imagine that naked need earlier? He's pulled back whatever he was feeling and locked it away inside of him.

It confuses me, this conflict I sense in him. He wants me, yet he hates himself for wanting me. He's trying to stop what he feels for me, and I don't understand why.

He stretches out a hand and when I take it, he pulls me to my feet. For a second, I am close to him again. Close enough to feel the heat from his body. Close enough to see the creases at the edge of his eyes.

He reaches out, brushing my hair from my forehead.

I start at that.

"You're hurt," he says.

I touch my forehead and wince when it sparks off a pulse of pain. My fingers come away wet with blood.

Then I see past him to the smoldering ruins of my studio and forget everything else.

"The vampire," I say, and my voice comes out weak. "He planted an explosive in there."

"He was trying to kill you. Do you know why? What did he want?" he asks.

His arm comes around my shoulder, the gesture purely meant to comfort, and I don't resist.

It's not the first time the vampires have come after me. And as it gets closer to the blood moon, their attacks have only grown more frequent. They want the sword *and me*. If they capture me, they'll harness the power of the sword for their own selfish needs.

I'll never allow that to happen. I'd die before I let them use me.

But I don't tell him this.

Then a thought strikes me and I gasp. "The orphans," I say, my throat closing with fear. "I need to check that they are safe."

"The orphans?" he asks, his voice puzzled, but already I am brushing past him, heading for the road.

"I fight to get money for the orphanage," I fling over my shoulder as he follows me. "It's already been attacked once before by the vampires. I need to make sure the children are safe."

"That's why you cage-fight?" he asks, sounding surprised. Then, quickening his pace, he pulls ahead of me. "My bike is not far. I'll take you."

I wonder then, why someone who barely knows me is going out of his way to help me.

"How did you find me?" I ask.

My eyes go to the tattoo peeking up the neck of his shirt. I guess the reason but want to hear it from him, anyway.

"I needed a tattoo," he obliges. "*You* run a tattoo studio."

A convenient explanation.

Too convenient.

I resist looking back at the wreckage.

The studio was the one place I could express myself. Give

form to the essence I sensed in those around me. It hadn't been much, but it had been mine.

All gone.

"I suppose I should be thankful I survived." I try to make light of the situation, but my voice comes out all shaky.

"I don't know," he says. "Sometimes death is easier than life."

I shoot a sharp glance at him, wondering what he meant by that. But he doesn't say anything more.

Perhaps I am not the only one with a death wish.

Reaching the bike he kick-starts it, nodding to me to hop on.

I pause, hesitant, and then ask the question that has bothered me all along.

"You jumped into the cage to save my life. Why?" I ask. "Why would you do that?"

"You kissed me earlier," he replies, his voice bland. "Why did you do *that*?"

I have no reply.

The wolf in me trusts him, and the woman in me can't resist him. Even though I know he's not telling me the real reason for coming to the studio today.

It can't be only to get a tattoo. Had he come in search of me? Had he felt the connection between us earlier in the ring?

I look into those silver-green eyes gleaming at me, knowing he's not even human.

Who is he?

I want to ask him, but don't. Right now, I'm too shaken from the fight with the vamp, from the studio being blown up. Besides, I need to get to the orphanage, make sure the kids are okay. And he can take me there.

"Leana," I hold out my hand.

He takes it, his palm dwarfing mine.

"Mikhail," he replies.

His voice shivers over my skin, sinking in, setting off sparks in their wake.

His grip is strong, firm. His thumb caresses the pulse hammering at my wrist. I tremble.

His eyes fix on mine, the silver in them glinting. An answering heat swirls in my belly.

Then a shutter falls over them and he turns away, dropping my palm. The mask is back. Once more, I sense the coiled intent in him. Does he intend to use my reaction against me?

I know then I can't stop him from taking whatever he wants from me. I also can't stop wondering why I feel this way for someone I barely know.

CHAPTER 8

As Mikhail drives up the road, my arms creep around his waist, feeling the solid muscles under his shirt.

His skin would be soft with an underlying toughness. And beneath it all, I sense a core of something strong. Something steady drawing me, making me want to explore. He too has secrets and I want to find out what they are.

I won't rest till I do.

I can't resist. I give in and open myself up to him. Open my senses and 'see' him. I gasp when the heat from him floods into me. It swirls around me and sinks into my skin. And the patterns! I see deep-green circles. Silver lines run through the center of each, connecting them to form a hexagonal figure.

Nothing like the muted colors that bleed from humans or shifters. Even as they flow over me, I remember where I've seen this design—in sacred geometry texts donated to the orphanage.

I'd been fascinated by its shape and colors. By how the structure represents the unseen: the mysteries of the world beyond.

Now seeing it leap to life, its sheer clarity, the way it glows with an otherworldly light…I know he can't be human.

Even as I think that, the entire unit pulses violet and revolves, and in the center of it is Mikhail.

Then, I spot it.

A silver cord leads out of him. It's thin, ethereal, newly

formed. Light glistens off it as I follow it back, following as it runs to me. Right into my womb. Joining me to him.

My eyes fly open, and I must have gasped aloud, for he half-turns and asks over his shoulder, "Are you all right?"

I don't reply.

I can't.

Can't even begin to make sense of what I have seen.

The wolf in me has already reached out to him, plugged into him. My animal has initiated a mating bond with him. I hadn't even been aware of it.

As that thought crosses my mind, my hands drop from around his waist. I lean back, trying to put distance between us. But I can't go far on the narrow seat.

Instead, I fold my arms over my chest. My forearms brush against his back. I feel his muscles stiffen.

He speeds up some more, sudden enough that I am jolted forward and have to hold onto him for support. My palms grip his waist again, and I try to keep the touch impersonal. *Ha! As if!*

"Turn off here," I say, relieved that we are almost at the orphanage on the western side of the city, at the edge of Juhu Beach.

Then we clear the trees, turning the corner from where the orphanage is visible. All thoughts go out of my head.

"No!" I exclaim, taking in the devastation in front of me.

The agony I felt at the destruction of the tattoo studio is nothing compared to the terror running through me now.

Before he has stopped the bike, I've climbed off. I run toward the smoking ruins of a building that once housed close to a hundred children.

No. No. No.

My mind feels like it's stuck in a loop, not wanting to believe the orphanage is hit.

Running up the driveway, we pass a volunteer's body, face down in the mud. Blood stains the grass around him.

I slow down and would have stopped, but Mikhail half-drags me along. I can't take my eyes off the figure.

"Nothing you can do for him," he says, his voice rough.

I am about to protest, but he's right. The man is gone. We pass more bodies, and this time I don't stop to look. Don't look at the toys scattered around. And then it's his turn to slow down. He halts by the books half-buried in the mud and curses aloud.

I know what he's thinking. Paper books are rare, all but extinct. And now these too are gone.

I slide my arm free of him and slam my fist into his middle, so the breath rushes out of him.

He barely even feels it.

It's more the suddenness of my attack that makes him frown. He shackles his fingers around my wrist.

"What's wrong with you?" he asks.

"*What's wrong with you?*" I yell back. "You care about books more than life?" My eyes spark fire at him.

Tears stream down my cheeks. I barely see him for the emotions churning inside.

"When you live as long as me," he says, "death is a welcome release." His voice is hard. "But children?" The silver in his eyes burns. He looks lethal. His body thrums with a violence that screams he's dangerous. "They are innocent." He says. "What the vampires did is unforgivable." His words are harsh, that clipped accent more pronounced.

"If I could, I'd exchange my life for theirs," I say.

His grip on my arm tightens, squeezing till it hurts.

"Don't say that," he snaps, and I stare, surprised by his outburst. So, he's not as aloof as he'd like me to believe.

He cares about the kids.

He cares about me.

Those green eyes of his flare. In their swirling depths, I see anger and confusion.

"I should have been here to save them." My voice emerges broken.

"Don't," Mikhail says. "Don't punish yourself. It's not your fault."

But of course, it is.

I'd promised to care of the orphans and I'd failed.

"You have no idea what you are talking about," I say.

He leans in, a strange look on his face. It's like he's being torn apart inside. He doesn't want to show me any gentleness, doesn't want to show he cares, and yet he can't help himself.

He touches his forehead to mine.

His gentleness is my undoing. Tears held back run unchecked. He feels so large and safe in this world gone crazy. I stop myself from reaching out to him.

His very resilience seems to make me weak, and right now I must stay strong.

So, I pull away from him. And look up as a gust of wind blows away the rest of the smoke.

That's when I see Grandmaster Aki.

CHAPTER 9

AKI STANDS BY THE BURNING building, his beard rippling in the breeze. Steel-grey hair, the same color as his beard, falls to his shoulders. Normally his frame is tall, erect. Today, he looks fragile.

His shirt is stained with dirt and blood. Seeing him, a rush of warmth—a feeling I reserve for Aki—washes over me.

He's alive!

I sprint up the driveway toward him.

"What happened to Rohan? And the children?" I cry out.

The vibrations from my voice must have disturbed the building, for a creak shudders through the ground. The structure caves in on itself.

I scream and rush toward Aki. He's closer to the falling bricks, and I'm sure he's going to be hurt. But Mikhail beats me to it.

Grabbing the still shell-shocked Aki, Mikhail throws him over his shoulder and turns.

"Run, Leana!"

I obey him without a second thought. Turning, I run in the direction we came from.

By the time I reach the road, Mikhail is already there. *And he was carrying a grown man.*

As he lowers Aki to the ground, I'm struck by the width of

Mikhail's shoulders, the flex of his biceps. He towers over Aki, making the older man seem almost childlike in contrast. Yet, his touch is gentle, his movements unhurried. He makes sure Aki is stable on his feet before stepping back.

Mikhail's gaze swivels to me and I redden, knowing I was staring. When he turns away, I follow his eyes to the now collapsed orphanage and stifle a cry.

Where the building once stood, there is now rubble. The debris is still on fire. The wind blows in our direction, bringing with it the smell of dust, smoke, and something else. Something pungent. The smell of burning flesh.

The children.

My stomach turns, and even as I swallow it down, I hear a broken sound. A gasp emerges from the man next to me.

"Aki!"

I close the gap between us and grip his shoulder, but he doesn't move.

He doesn't even look at me. Aki simply stares at the space where the orphanage once stood. At the life he built. The life he gave to those kids.

Aki survived the tsunami as a ten-year-old. Lived through the invasion by the hybrids, the formation of the Council and what they did to rip the soul from the city. He found his calling in this orphanage. Like me.

Gone. All gone. Destroyed by the vampires.

It strikes me then how fleeting life is.

"Aki," I say again, my voice gentle. "What happened?"

He turns to me. Blinks.

"The vampires took the shifter kids," he says. "The volunteers and I tried to defend the children, but even our trained fighters were no match. The vampires killed the humans, then,

42

set the orphanage on fire."

His voice is flat, hard, like he's reading out facts.

"I only just managed to save myself." He sways and I notice the side of his shirt is drenched in blood. He's hurt. I grip his shoulder, supporting him.

Sickness twists my stomach.

"Rohan." Aki swallows, a look of pain flashing across his face. "He did it. He's working with the vampires."

Aki's eyes are unseeing, unable to grasp what's happening around him.

"Rohan?"

No. I don't believe it.

I always sensed that darker edge to my cousin, but not that he would hurt the kids. He couldn't be this heartless, could he?

Another shudder from the building as the last remaining wall collapses. It sends a fresh burst of sparks shooting up in the air. The heat from the flames flares toward us, forcing us to take a few more steps back.

Without taking his eyes off the burning embers, Aki says, his voice harsh, "You should have tried to save more of the kids."

I am about to reply when Mikhail cuts in with, "They were already dead." His voice is matter of fact.

He's right of course, yet I wince on hearing them.

A tremor runs through Aki, and I tighten my hold on him.

"Stay with us, Aki, we need you here," I say, then add in a soft voice, "*I* need you here."

As I hear my words, I realize it's true. I do still need him. This man has been more than a father to me.

He'd been there for those orphans too, had given shelter to both shifters and humans alike. Unlike the Council, which relegates shifters to Shifter Town.

Aki was also the first person I had seen when trying to cross over into the main island of Bombay. What I noticed even then was his presence. Real, vital, he thrived on the life force of this city.

Now seeing his eyes flat, I am filled with fear. I've never seen him this broken. Not even when his wife, Veena, had died.

Not like this.

Aki gestures to me.

"We must save them before the vampires take their life force, Leana." His voice rises in fear.

"So you, an aging grandmaster and she, a lone shifter, are going to take on the vampires?" Mikhail asks.

His voice is angry, eyes narrowed with surprise and … something else. Fear. He's afraid if I go after the kids, I will get hurt.

And that surprises me. He's feeling more than he's letting on.

Aki's gaze sweeps over Mikhail. His forehead furrows, trying to place the younger man. A look of recognition coming into his eyes.

"But we are not alone, are we?" Aki says. "You are going to help us. Took your time getting here though, didn't you?"

I look from him to Mikhail, not quite understanding what he means. On Mikhail's face, the same surprise I feel.

"What do you mean, old man?" Mikhail asks.

And then Aki does something unexpected. He throws his head back and laughs.

CHAPTER 10

DANIEL SPRAWLS ON THE PLUSH sofa in his bungalow.

The moonlight shimmering in through the open window kisses Daniel's dark blonde hair.

"Did you *have* to destroy the orphanage?" Rohan snaps. "You could have spared the human children, at least."

Eyes wary, Daniel watches Rohan pace the room.

"At least they died for a larger cause," Daniel replies. "Not everyone is so fortunate."

The melody in his voice marks him out instantly as being of Spanish origin. A deep, rich voice that has lulled many into a false sense of security. But Daniel knows it'll take more than a seductive tone to calm Rohan down. Daniel's not even sure why it's so important that he appease this boy.

Yet, he can't stop himself from adding. "Bring me the sword and no one else needs to be hurt. Besides, you chose your path a while ago." His tone toughens as he remembers how Rohan had insisted Daniel help him. "Or have you forgotten it was you who wanted the vampires to attack the orphanage the first time?"

Rohan's fists clench at his side. "That was different," he says. "It was to get Matteo out of my way. Too bad I didn't kill him before Leana got there."

At Leana's name, Daniel stiffens.

Rohan mutters, "Leana killed him, and now she'll never

forget him. But this time, I won't make the same mistake." Rohan exhales. "I'm going to kill the male she lusts after myself."

When Rohan runs his fingers through his hair, Daniel is surprised to see them trembling.

Rohan is talking about the woman he's fixated on. He's making it clear to Daniel that he doesn't stand a chance with Rohan.

Yet, this sign of vulnerability makes Rohan more attractive to Daniel. His growing feelings for Rohan, also make Daniel feel vulnerable. And *that* Daniel does not like.

He drinks from his whiskey glass and the tart taste heightens the feeling of his life being out of control.

The last time Daniel felt this exposed was when he'd been swept away by the tsunami. He'd woken, naked and shivering, to a world gone crazy. He'd been one of the closest to the Trombay nuclear reactor, a scientist with a promising research career, and a young wife and child. All gone. Swept away by the wave.

Leaving behind him: a mutated specimen.

Even now, the transformation feels unreal.

But as he looks around his richly furnished bungalow, at this second life he's built for himself, it strikes Daniel that if he had not become a vampire, he'd not have all this.

The bungalow perches on a cliff on an outlying island. Set beyond the seven main islands of Bombay, Daniel bought the island outright. As a vampire, he has everything his human self wanted: wealth and a near immortal life.

He also has the kind of strength he never dreamed of, both physical and mental strength.

He has everything but the ability to father more of his species.

The one flaw in vampires is they can't reproduce with others of their kind. Daniel's decades of experiments led him to conclude it's because vampire genes are too perfect.

To propagate, vampires need to balance the cold logic so inherent in them with the emotions of shifters. For this, Daniel must take a female shifter as mate.

Rohan's not a shifter. And of course, being male, he can't help Daniel in propagating his species.

Yet, Daniel can't stop wanting this man. The way Rohan makes him feel transcends logic.

Daniel has lived long enough have taken females and males of different species as partners. But he can't remember feeling so drawn to anyone else. Not even to his dead human wife.

Now as his eyes fall on the younger man, a familiar heat licks his lower belly. The shiver of muscles under Rohan's skin as he moves, his sculpted chest, his flat waist ... Daniel's eyes moves lower.

Rohan's eyes widen, those indigo swirls catching the bright starlight. One side of his lips rises in the makings of a smile.

Walking toward Daniel, Rohan picks up the vampire's drink. Takes a sip.

"Neat whiskey?" Rohan grimaces. "It tastes like charcoal."

Daniel chuckles at his disgust.

"Peat. It has a peat smoke flavor," Daniel says, his lips curving.

He can almost taste the bittersweet swirl of the aged whiskey in Rohan's mouth. He wonders how it would taste on Rohan's tongue.

Daniel's eyes drop to Rohan's lips. His lower lip juts out a little. In his head, he sees Rohan as a young boy, stubborn, adamant. He would have been hell to deal with.

Then Rohan's tongue slides out, licking off the remaining drops of the liquor from his lips. A flash of heat tightens Daniel's groin. He wants to fit his mouth there. Wants to run his nails down that flash of skin exposed between the open ends of his unbuttoned shirt, that tough, yet creamy, almost-hairless chest.

Rohan places the whiskey glass back in Daniel's cupped palm. He doesn't let go though, so when Daniel pulls the glass toward him, Rohan comes with it, too. Bending from the waist, his body sinks in toward Daniel, close. Closer still.

All that separates them is the width of the glass.

Rohan's so close that the heat from his skin slams into Daniel, making him wince. That musk and cumin smell that is so Rohan sinks into him. A bittersweet reminder that Daniel can't have Rohan. It taunts him, coils around him, pulls at him.

Daniel raises the glass—and Rohan's hand wrapped around it—to his lips. Without taking his eyes off Rohan, he lowers his face and licks Rohan's fingers.

A palpable shiver runs through Rohan.

So, Rohan's not completely unaffected. Rohan may not share his taste in the male of the species, but he is not completely immune to Daniel's charm either.

Sensing the thoughts running through Daniel. Perhaps realizing he's revealed more than he's comfortable with, Rohan lets go of the glass.

Straightening, Rohan walks away, giving Daniel a full view of that tight behind. He glides with a half-swagger that's so male, it's almost feminine.

Molten heat spurts in Daniel's lower belly, hardening him to the point he has to adjust himself.

By the time Rohan reaches the window where he had been leaning against earlier, Daniel has sat up.

His arm rests loosely on his knee glass in hand. Wiping all emotion off his face, Daniel asks, "So, have you given my proposition further thought?"

CHAPTER 11

"You mean will I get you the sword?" Rohan asks. "You want me to go against everything my father stood for?" He sounds bitter.

"You miss him?"

Rohan hesitates, then chooses his words with care: "Jai's way of life was one of duty, of putting the city first before anything else. Before his own family, even. It's not something I ever understood," he says. "Ariana loved him." Rohan's voice softens when he speaks of his mother. "She'd have died for him. And Jai loved Ariana, too. Yet, he preferred to die for his city."

"You are very like her, aren't you?" Daniel remarks.

It's the first time in the months they have known each other that Rohan has spoken openly about his parents.

Daniel wonders if distance has put more perspective on Rohan's relationship with them.

Has being away from everything familiar made Rohan realize the importance of what he had? The feeling of family, of being together, a unit against the world. Perhaps Rohan misses it.

Daniel realizes he wants the same feeling with Rohan. And as soon as he thinks that, his grip tightens on the glass.

Rohan goes on. "It's ironic that it is thanks to my parents we met. If Jai hadn't been killed, if Ariana had not taken over as Mayor and called you to the table to negotiate in secret, if you hadn't accepted and come to the Mayoral mansion—"

"If you hadn't opened the door to me to let me in..." Daniel completes Rohan's statement.

If he hadn't been working at the Atomic Centre when the tsunami had struck... Daniel pushes the thought away.

He places his glass on the table.

Supporting his elbows on his thighs, he steeples his fingers and rests his chin on them.

"There are no coincidences in life, dear boy—" Daniel starts to say, only to be interrupted by Rohan.

"Don't call me a boy. I am not as old as you, but am not that young either."

The flash of annoyance sends another pulse of heat through Daniel. He clamps down on it. What the fuck is wrong with him?

He even finds Rohan's anger endearing.

Is he falling in love with the boy? The thought brings him up short.

Rohan is special all right, and not only for his pedigree as the son of the Mayor of Bombay.

Daniel raises his palm face up, stopping Rohan from speaking. "Do you know how unique your aura is, Ro? You follow your instincts, not caring about the world. If I could, I'd bathe myself in your light. I'd drink it. Drink of you."

Drink your life-force. Make you mine.

Daniel doesn't say that aloud, of course.

Rohan's energy brings out a psychic hunger in Daniel that takes him by surprise.

It also worries him. Makes him wonder what hold the boy has on him.

He was attracted to Rohan from the beginning, but this need to take Rohan's essence, to possess him body and soul is new.

Psychic vampires sucked the essence from their victims till they died.

But when the victim was allowed to live, it also became an act that left a lasting bond between the two.

He'd always been attracted to Rohan, but this deepening of his feelings takes Daniel by surprise.

Some of his emotions must show on his face for Rohan goes pale. A blush stains his cheeks. Then that too is gone. His jaw hardens, indigo eyes going stormy. He opens his mouth to speak. But Daniel is the first to get his words in.

"I could ask you to sleep with me knowing you cannot refuse, but I won't," he says. "I won't ask you to bare yourself to me. Or how much I want to feel the your skin as it slides over mine."

His voice winds its way across the room, reaching out to Rohan.

But Rohan doesn't react. He watches Daniel, his stance alert.

"I won't ask you to do any of that, for I know your preferences lie in the female of the species," Daniel says.

Rohan's features relax a little at that.

"Not that it will stop me from imagining what I want to do to you." Daniel half-jokes.

"Daniel," Rohan warns.

The vampire nods, folding his arms over his chest.

"Which brings me to my original train of thought before you distracted me," Daniel says with a chuckle.

His smile widens when Rohan shakes his head at the flirtatious tone.

"I don't want you to go against your family. But you're not a boy anymore, as you so correctly pointed out. Choose then. Become a man. Own the direction you want your life to take," he says. "Can you do that?"

Daniel lets the words hang in the space between them. Going back to his drink, he drains it before placing the glass back on the table with a snap.

"The girl, I want her," Rohan says, his voice so low that initially Daniel's not even sure he's heard the words.

But then the full meaning of it sinks in, and Daniel's eyes narrow.

"Leana," Rohan says. "Hand her over to me and you get the sword."

"Your cousin?" Daniel's features tighten.

He knew Rohan slept with women, and he didn't care about that. But this is different. There's a near obsession with the female in Rohan's voice. Daniel's gut twists with an emotion he can't quite put his finger on. *Jealousy*. Yes, that's what it is.

It slashes through him, digging into him till he's sure the pain shows on his face. He wonders if his facade is going to shatter, if he's finally going to be revealed for what he's become: A lovesick loser.

Of course, before that can happen, his vampire self, the one he has spent years training, takes over. It crushes the emotions shattering them into nothingness. Then that too is promptly absorbed.

Daniel is back then as he intends to be seen.

Cold.

Emotionless.

Hungry

He pushes aside his feelings for Rohan. "You can have her. But first, get me the sword," he says, voice harsh.

CHAPTER 12

I WANTED TO SET OFF in search of the children right away, but neither Aki nor Mikhail was sure where they could have been taken. I couldn't figure out where to start, either.

Mikhail had suggested we stop by his place and see to our wounds. He wanted to regroup and come up with a plan before we went in search of the orphans.

He's being sensible about it.

I know he's right and yet a part of me resents having to bide my time. It's already nightfall, and the days' events have wrung me out. Even if we knew where we'd been heading, we wouldn't have gone far before we'd have to rest.

But, with every minute that passes, the chances of finding the children alive decreases. Even thinking of it makes my insides churn with fear.

When Aki too had sided with Mikhail I'd been surprised. But by then, I could barely think straight with exhaustion. Aki was in pain and looked so fragile, I knew there was no way we could continue with him in this state.

So, I pretended to give in. I had every intention of creeping away at night once everyone had fallen asleep.

Besides, I wanted to find out what Aki knew about Mikhail.

So here we are.

In Mikhail's bungalow.

Devein dresses Aki's wounds, his touch gentle, movements quick. After he finishes with Aki, he turns to me. When it's Mikhail's turn, he lets Devein fuss over him.

Mikhail seems to understand that Devein will feel better if he has the chance to take care of him.

It makes me wonder again about Mikhail's hidden depths. He prefers to mask his feelings behind those near perfect features, which give very little away.

After Devein finishes, Mikhail stands by the large window of his living room. Half-turned away from us, he looks out to the beach. The ebb and flow of the waves in the distance should be soothing, but it feels ominous.

Standing there on his own, his stern profile in repose, the loneliness from him bleeds out.

Perhaps his emotions reach me through the emerging mating bond; I can taste the bleakness of his past. The need to comfort him is so strong that I am on my feet, crossing the room toward him, before I even realize what I'm doing.

When I touch his shoulder, he flinches, before turning around. In the background, the skies blush pink from the setting sun.

"I'll help you find the children, Leana," he says. "I am not as heartless as you think me to be." His voice is serious.

I know that already. But I don't let on.

"There's something you should know first." He hesitates.

Those silver-green eyes glow with an inner light. I know then, he's going to tell me more about his past. A feeling of dread grips me and suddenly I don't want to hear this.

Mikhail grasps my shoulder and I sense he's trying to comfort me.

"So, are you finally going to tell her who you are, boy?" Aki asks.

Mikhail chuckles, the sound harsh.

"Who am I?" he asks. "Other than a person who doesn't know his origins? Someone with no memories of his past, nothing beyond the time he's spent in this house, in this city." He cuts the air with his hand, a confident gesture, one of negation, one of pushing aside the obvious. A gesture I am beginning to recognize already.

"Besides, I am scarcely a boy." He turns to me and waits.

Waits for me to ask the obvious question.

"How old are you, Mikhail?" I can't stop myself.

He replies, his voice flat, "In human years, much older than you. I believe I am almost a hundred and seventeen years."

"No way!" I exclaim, unable to keep the surprise out of my voice.

"I may not remember who tried to kill me, but apparently, I have enough innate knowledge to figure out my age." His tone is self-deprecating.

I only half hear him, trying to make sense of what he's saying. I can't stop looking at him, either.

At the thick black-brown hair framing sharp cheekbones. The corded neck leading to wide shoulders with well-formed muscles. I know, because I'd felt the hard length of his chest and that almost concave stomach, which fit so neatly over my curves.

A dense swirl of heat from him reaches out to me. He's aware of what I'm seeing in my head.

What I am imagining.

Us.

I take a step back, ignoring the slight twist of his lips. He knows I'm putting space between us.

"And in terms of your own species...I mean, wherever you

come from." My voice falters, as I struggle to grasp what my heart has already accepted. What my wolf doesn't even question. What I had glimpsed earlier along with the mating cord.

He's not of this earth.

"I age at approximately one-fourth the rate of the human race," he says, "which puts me at thirty-three years, in terms of my species."

"What species is that?" I blurt out.

Seeing him pale at the question, I bite my lips. Perhaps it had been indiscreet of me to ask.

"I don't know." He bows his head, shoulders slumping.

It's the first time I've seen him unsure of anything. All this time, he'd been confident, arrogant even. Now to see him struggle to explain his origins—it's the first sign of weakness I have seen in him.

And *that* makes him feel more human.

Then Aki says, his voice soft, "Whoever you are, you're our savior, Mikhail."

Silence.

Mikhail walks over to the wall, to where I'd been standing earlier. It's his turn to want to put space between himself and the rest of us. He leans against it, his pose almost mirroring mine.

"Next you'll tell me I am divine." He laughs without humor.

"What if you are?" Aki replies.

Devein takes a sharp breath, and my throat closes. I knew it all along, ever since he first jumped in that cage and put himself between me and the shifter male.

No ordinary man would have risked his life like that. Confident in the knowledge he couldn't be hurt.

I also recall how Mikhail had carried Aki and not even been out of breath. Remember that violet and green hexagon with

Mikhail at its center. Those colors and shapes come to life from the books of sacred geometry. This can mean only one thing: he is not of this earth.

The human in me still refuses to believe it, but my wolf knows. My wolf has accepted that otherworldliness in him.

Unlike shifters or vampires, he wasn't the product of genetic modification. He was created this way.

The emotions flickering inside must have shown on my face for Aki nods at me, agreeing.

"You were washed upon these shores for a reason," he tells Mikhail. "Surely you must know that by now."

Mikhail folds his hands over his chest and stands straight, ramrod stiff. His jaw hardens and his gaze goes shuttered. I have a glimpse of what he must've been in that past life of his: a soldier who refused to bow down, who fought for his people.

Will he stay and fight for us now?

"I know I'm different, and it's not something I want or asked for," Mikhail says, his voice hard. "Do you know what it is to spend each waking day wondering where you came from? Wondering who you had left behind. Puzzled when you don't age like the others, as you see your friends age before your eyes?"

I follow his gaze toward Devein, who has a fierce look on his face. Devein knows how Mikhail feels right now. Feels the confusion and hurt. I am sure Devein has known all along that Mikhail is not like other humans.

"Can't you leave him be?" Devein directs his anger at Aki, his voice stretched. Devein would do anything to protect this man. Mikhail's more than a friend, he's family.

"So all these years, you knew you had these abilities ..." I turn to Mikhail. "Yet you didn't do anything to help humans or the shifters as the vampires began to prey on us?"

"Why should he save those who were responsible for beating him up, throwing him overboard to die?" Devein shoots back.

"The shifters did that?" I ask shocked. Shifters are violent creatures, some prefer to give in to the animal side more than others.

Mikhail stays quiet, yet his anger is palpable. I know then it's true. A sense of disbelief descends. No wonder he hates shifters.

How can I expect him to feel anything for me, when my kind is responsible for overturning his life?

"Doesn't mean we are all like that." I force the words out through a throat gone dry.

"You need to look beyond this," Aki tells Mikhail, his voice quiet. "You have allowed this world to distract you enough. It's made you lose track of who you are. But now we need you. You are the one we've been waiting for."

"You sound so confident," I say. "Almost like a prediction." I laugh, a nervous sound.

I am the only one.

There's no trace of humor in Aki's voice when he says, "It *was* a prediction. Brahma himself told me so."

"Brahma, our founding father?" I ask.

Aki was one of the original children rescued by Brahma from the floods following the 2014 tsunami. But in all the time I've known Aki, he's never mentioned this.

"Brahma was a seer," Aki replies. "It's why he was chosen to re-populate the new world. He knew there were many possibilities in the future. The tsunami had changed the balance of the universe, introducing new species. It altered the shape of evolution.

"He knew some of the creations could not be allowed to run astray. That there had to be checks and balances.

"Even then, Brahma had sensed that the tsunami was only the start. That great evil would follow in its footsteps. He knew the darkness in the form of vampires would come. That they'd prey on humans and shifters, take their emotional life force in their thirst to survive.

"He also predicted the coming of a savior. Someone washed ashore, one with no past, and not of this earth." Aki pauses. "A being more intelligent than humans, stronger than shifters, and more potent than even vampires in his psychic abilities."

Silence fills the room as we take it all in. Mikhail's face is shuttered, careful as he watches Aki. He's not even surprised by what Aki is saying.

"What do you mean, Aki?" I ask, my voice impatient.

Aki turns his wise eyes on me, on his lips a slight smile. "Brahma predicted that when evil reaches its darkest hour, this being, one of the avatars of the divine, will appear. In this reincarnation, the immortal will join forces with the wolf." He looks at me pointedly. "Wielding a flaming sword, together, they strike at the heart of darkness, banishing it forever.

"I believe he was talking about the two you," he says, his voice serious. "Question is, can you save us?" He addresses the question to me before turning his full attention to Mikhail. "Do you *want* to save us?"

CHAPTER 13

MIKHAIL STANDS ON THE DECK outside his ground floor bedroom. It leads down to the garden and beyond that, the beach. In his hand is a glass of whiskey.

Tomorrow morning they'll be off. Right after Aki revealed the predictions, he also said that their best bet to look for the vampires would be to ask the Council about it.

He's known for some time that the Council had been in secret negotiations with the vampires. They'd been in touch with Daniel, the vampire leader. It had to be Daniel who was behind the kidnapping of the children.

They had agreed to set off for the Council headquarters at dawn.

All this was after Aki had mentioned that he thought Mikhail was divine.

Mikhail had thought himself to be many things over the years, but to call himself divine feels far-fetched. He knew his psychic design abilities were extraordinary, that he wasn't hundred percent human. But a part of him had never stopped hoping. *The part that still wants to fit in.*

Or perhaps he'd tired of watching humans and their lives from the sidelines. Perhaps seeing Leana has made him realize that at heart he wanted the same things as them.

Things he hadn't acknowledged even to himself.

He wants her, wants a life with her... wanted children. For the first time, Mikhail admits he wants his own family. Wants to belong to something larger than himself. Wants to create more than code. With Leana, he wants to create life.

For the first time in his long life, one in which he's often wished himself dead, Mikhail wants the opposite. He wants to feel alive. To feel Leana's body come live under him.

When he jumped into the ring to save her, he altered the course of his destiny.

And he hadn't even realized it.

Leana has awakened unfamiliar desires. Even acknowledging all this confuses him.

Is it just lust, or something deeper that binds them? Something fated?

He swears aloud, the harsh sound torn from his lips by the wind blowing in from the Arabian Sea.

He touches his tongue to his lips. It comes away salty from the breeze.

It reminds him of the taste of Leana's lips. Tart yet sweet. Like the emotions he feels swirling inside her now, even when she's not in the same space as him.

When it comes to Leana, he has a finely attuned radar that can track her wherever she is.

It confounds him, that he can even now sense her presence. No matter where she is, if he lowers the barrier of his mind and reaches out to her, he can feel her.

His inner light, the one he keeps so closely guarded, unwinds. It spools out across the distance, down the corridor to the room Devein had shown her to earlier.

When he feels her flinch Mikhail promptly withdraws. He pulls his light into himself, curling it back in that space deep inside him.

He feels this need to protect her. Make sure she is safe. Make sure she didn't go the way of the woman with indigo eyes. That he didn't lose her a second time.

He realizes with a start that Leana's face has begun replacing that of the woman of his dreams. Her amber eyes pushing out the indigo ones. The image that had seen him through all those years. All those nights when he had lain awake and wondered who he really was.

All he had then were those indigo eyes. But not anymore.

Not since Leana.

Leana is his now, his future.

And the other woman? She belongs to the past, to the person he had once been.

It feels wrong to let go of the vision that has given him hope all this time. But Mikhail knows he must, for he has no choice.

Swearing aloud, he tosses the rest of the whiskey back, welcoming its burn.

Turning, he walks into his room, placing the glass on the table. His movements are controlled. Too controlled. The restraint in his actions gives away the anger bubbling inside.

He moves toward the violin in its case, next to the table. His hand comes away dusty. It's been months...years even since he's last held it. But today, it feels right to pick it up and play.

Stepping back onto the balcony, he fits the violin under his chin and draws the bow. He lets himself sink into the notes, letting it wash over him, till it sets his mind free to think.

His mind mulls what Aki had said. Is he divine or a freak? A messenger of God perhaps? Or one sent by the devil to do his bidding?

Often Mikhail can't distinguish which side he belongs to. He presses the bow down, and the snapping of the string twangs a broken melody that shocks his eyes open.

"And I thought only we shifters had trouble keeping emotions under control?" Leana's mocking voice brings him up short.

Lowering the violin, Mikhail tries to get a grip on the thoughts running through his head.

But he's too aware her presence. The breeze from the open sea ruffles his hair. Goose bumps rise on his skin.

Since he saw the vamp leap at her and take her down, saw her bleed; since then, something had loosened inside. Something knotted inside of him had simply dissolved. Now he can't stop himself from wanting her.

He wants this female shifter and not only her body. He wants to possess her mind and soul. He wants to bury himself in her, drink of her essence, and never let her go.

The thought makes him step away from her, putting distance between them.

He doesn't need to hear the quick exhale of her breath to know he's hurt her.

"Do you believe in destiny, Mikhail?" She asks, her voice so soft he can barely hear her.

"No." He shakes his head, his features closed. "I believe in chance"

CHAPTER 14

HIS MUSIC ... THOSE PLAINTIVE NOTES had woken me up from my restless sleep.

Before I came fully awake, I was out of the door, walking down the corridor and toward where the music was coming from.

I opened the room and walked toward the balcony before I saw him. His back was to the door, shoulders slightly hunched, the violin cradled in his arms like it was a woman... or something more precious. *He was playing out the memories of his past life.*

Walking past the bookshelf loaded with books—paper books, expensive to come by in this new world—I continued, drawn toward him. Unable to resist the lament of his music.

Hearing it made me hurt. Twisted my heart with an agony I couldn't quite place.

I hadn't believed it was Mikhail playing, that the heart-wrenchingly beautiful notes were from him. Not till I saw it with my own eyes. My gaze traveled over those broad shoulders, the muscles of his arms flexing as he played. Head in profile, eyelids shuttered down over those high cheekbones as sharp as the strings over which he swept his bow.

Perhaps because I was still half-asleep, I was open, heart and soul open, and reached out to him.

I could see his essence spool out, reach out to me, curl

around me, and pull me to him.

And I had gone.

To him.

I'd wanted him. Until now when his words shatter something inside. Yet, I mustn't show it. Not now. Not when that fragile bond between us is beginning to form.

He pulls away from me, and I know it's because he's reminded yet again that I am a shifter.

I feel the tension vibrating off him, mixed with something else. Pain. *Loss.*

This man has lost something very close to him. Perhaps even lost himself. I know now shifters are the cause of it. No wonder he hates my kind. *Does he hate me too?*

He glances at me, eyes hooded. He wants to shut me out. But a part of him is drawn to me despite everything. It's like he's seeing me for the first time.

The silence drags on.

And on.

Finally, I point over my shoulder without turning. "So many books," I say, my voice coming out high, nervous.

His features stay shuttered.

Is he not going to answer me at all?

Then he speaks, his voice low. "When you're different from everyone else, when you don't know what you are, then you turn to books for answers."

"Is that what you did all these years?" I ask.

I never met my mother, and my father but once.

My pack-guardian had brought me up out of duty, and I never considered her my mother. Still, I'd always had pack-mates around me.

But Mikhail? He'd been truly alone, one of his kind. I can't even imagine how that must feel.

"I read. A lot," he admits. "And I learned to play the violin among other musical instruments."

"You also play other instruments?" I ask, stunned.

He nods, a quick jerk of the head. "You forget, I had a long time to master them." His tone is self-deprecating.

A cautious look creeps into his eyes. He's revealed more of himself and he's not comfortable with it.

"How's Aki?" he asks, abruptly changing the topic.

His voice is gruff, as he struggles to keep his emotions under control.

He looks tired, as exhausted as I feel right now.

The vamps had hit me where it hurt the most.

At my past.

In one stroke, they had made me face up to everything I had been running away from. But no more.

Tomorrow, we search for the children. But tonight … tonight.

It's time for me to face my feelings.

"Aki's shaken," I say, surprised when my voice comes out steady. That it doesn't reveal more of the turmoil running through me. "And so am I," I add. My voice soft, the words carried away on another gust of sea breeze.

He stiffens, his body going still.

I turn to him, looking at his profile, the sharp jut of his nose against the purple skies. My gaze follows across those high cheekbones and above them, those silvery, almost colorless eyes. He turns to me, and the breath catches in my throat.

I was mistaken. His eyes are not colorless. Quite the opposite, they take on the colors of the world around him. Of his emotions. Right now, they are pools of unsaid desires, unspoken words he wants to tell me but can't. *Won't.*

I reach out my finger and touch his cheek.

He winces but doesn't move away. He doesn't look at me, either. His eyes slide past, to fix on something beyond me. He can't bear to see me right now.

He's waiting. Waiting. Waiting for me to say something more. To do something.

He's waiting for me to reach out.

"Micah," I swallow, using his nickname.

He jerks, at the sound of my voice. Then sighs, the exhale warm, ruffling my hair. Goosebumps flare on my skin.

"What do you want, Leana?"

His voice shivers over my skin, tugging at my belly. Molten heat pours through me, and I tremble.

The explosion that ripped out my past and made me face up to my memories now demands that I accept what I feel for him.

Right now.

"I want you, Micah." The words tumble out.

I say it before I can change my mind. Say his name because it *has* to be him. I clench my fists at my side. The wolf in me wants to fling itself at him, seduce him. Take him. Ask him to take me.

Human that I am, I know I've made a mistake.

I'm sure the heat pouring out of him, slamming into my chest, is but my imagination. Sure his eyes that reflect the purple of the night skies don't mean anything. The tug I feel in my belly, that desire burning molten between my thighs, even as I stay poised in mid-flight, is…real.

I was mistaken. He won't let himself want me; he will not open himself to me.

I turn to go, and then he's there.

I don't even see him move. One moment he's behind me,

and the next he's right in front, so close his chest brushes mine. I have to tilt my head back to look at him. I raise my lips as he lowers his. And stops.

He stays there, staring into my eyes.

He's not touching me, not yet. Not physically. But desire leaps off him in a dense cloud that envelops me, tugs me. To him. That silver line, stretched tight between us, pulls at my womb, and it's my turn to shudder in surprise.

I thought I was ready, but now feeling the intensity of our connection, I am not so sure. If I take this step, I will be bound to him. Bound to a being who wants me, but yet hates my kind. He may never forgive me for what I am going to do tonight: for binding him to me.

But right now, I don't care.

All I know is I can't let him walk away from me.

Not now.

Not when I can see him...see us clearly.

Regardless of how much he resists and will not accept what we mean to each other, I am going to touch him, hold him. Forge him to me in the only way I know. The only way my wolf knows too.

Mikhail frowns, eyebrows slashing down. Then he yanks me to him.

CHAPTER 15

Sometimes everything fits.

Like now.

The heat from his skin pours over me, pulls at me, a living breathing thing. As live as Mikhail.

Shocked into stillness, I stand there, so close my waist touches him and he's already hard. I know then that he wants me. And that deepens this connection between us. Sends a pulse of molten craving through me. Shocking me. A part of me warns me to step back but I can't.

The rational part of me tries to understand what's happening between us. *Why am I reacting like this to someone I barely know?*

My senses flare open and just like that, his essence is there. That sparkling violet and green of him. I'm lost in him, for he's my mate. And now I can't resist.

Everything I feel for him rushes through. The past and future merge into one. Into this moment. Into us.

He feels it too, for his eyes widen. The color lightens, and they glow with a strange inner light. One I am beginning to recognize.

He nods, then leans into me.

I gasp, feeling like I've been physically hit.

I raise my lips and push my body into his. Wincing again when heat from him bleeds into me, I feel him thicken further. A jolt of molten desire runs through me...And *that's* when I realize then we haven't even started ... making love.

No, that's not true. These last few hours, he's been making love to me silently, with his eyes. It's been building and now I want to immerse myself in him. Let my wolf out to play. *Now.*

He slants his lips over mine and thrusts his tongue inside my mouth. Tasting me. Drinking of me. His hands on me. Over my back, down the slope of my hips, gripping me and then I am rising. Rising. My legs snake around his waist and, without taking his lips from my mouth, he walks to the bed, and then I am on my back.

Leaning down, he shocks me by tearing my shirt off in one go. I cry out in surprise, but he doesn't stop there. Doesn't stop till I am naked.

He plunges his finger inside me. One. Another. The palm of his other hand on my breast, squeezing. Then he leans down and bites the hardened nipple.

Desire shoots through me, almost blinding me. Before I can get ahold of myself, my lower body bucks, raising itself right off the bed and to my shock, I find myself climaxing right there.

And he still doesn't stop. It's like he wants to push me over the edge, not give me time to recover. *Or perhaps he likes to be in control so he doesn't have to show himself to me.*

The violence vibrates off him. I know he wants to break me, possess me, get me out of his system.

He has no idea how wrong he is, does he?

Then I stop thinking, for he covers my body with his.

And that's when I explode.

Everything pent up inside, from the time I saw Teo die, rushes through me, sinking deeper into me till I'm writhing under Mikhail.

I push the shirt off his shoulders, so I can knead his back, running my fingers over the furrows of his tattoos there.

He pulls back long enough to shuck his pants and then he captures my lips again, kissing me deeply. His tongue sliding over mine, and then he's inside me.

One moment I am empty, and the next he's there. It sends shock waves through me.

A jolt of pure silver flashes behind my eyes, blinding me. I am almost out of my head with wanting him. Heat courses through my veins, coating my body with perspiration.

But it's not enough.

Not nearly enough.

He's holding back. He still can't believe I—a shifter—can make him feel like this.

At that, anger pulses through me.

I want to push at him till he breaks. They way he broke through my defenses. Flinging my legs around his waist, I bury my fingers in his hair. Pull at his scalp till he groans into my mouth. The sound only inflames me further.

Tearing his mouth from me, he raises himself on his arms, biceps flexing on either side of my face. Another dense cloud of heat from his chest slams into me. I gasp, almost feverish with desire. Every part of me hurts.

We are not making love, but fighting each other.

His breath scorches my skin even as he trembles against me. When he looks into my eyes I am caught. Helpless. I can't look away. The glow in them deepens, light shining through glass. Fracturing into so many colors, I lose count. Fracturing me. He slams into me again. Sliding against my sensitive walls and sparking off jolts of longing. He groans, feeling it too, and that only fans the flames of my desire.

Grasping his hips with my thighs, my ankles entwined around him, I push myself up, wanting to get even closer. My entire body is wracked with such concentrated desire it's almost painful. I grip his arms, nails digging into his skin, hurting him, but he doesn't even seem to notice.

He pants, chest muscles rising-falling. Then angles himself and plunges still deeper. Goes right inside, so deep it feels like he's tearing me in half. The walls I've built around my wolf shiver. They vibrate with fear, with pleasure. Tight and tense. The wolf will not be held back. It leaps to meet its mate.

I scream.

In his eyes, I see myself reflected back.

Hear him groan as he comes inside me. Filling an emptiness I didn't even know existed. The sensations ripple through me, so intense I am yanked out of my body. I lose myself in our joined pleasure-pain.

WHEN I COME TO, HE'S looking at me. His eyes are back to being silvery-green, eyebrows lowered over his nose. I want to reach out and trace the crease on his near perfect forehead, but my arms are trapped somewhere under him.

He's large, virile, all around me, cocooning me in his warmth. Seducing me. Pulling me right back.

The connection between us already feels stronger, denser. It pulses with longing. Fed by our lovemaking, it's come alive.

Can he feel it too?

He must.

Heat tightens my lower belly. What happened between us has barely whetted my appetite. I want more. More of that feeling that had me breaking free, reaching for something I can't yet see. For a few seconds there, my wolf and me, we became one.

That thought makes me gasp in surprise. My eyelids flutter closed, but can still see his eyes, his lips; feel his skin on mine.

Mikhail is here. He's real.

And Teo's gone.

My need for Mikhail has only deepened in the last few hours with everything we'd been through. Shocking in its intensity, it feels all too real. It is real. This bond.

Because of that, I deny it. I still can't get my head around it. *How can you feel so much for someone you're just getting to know?*

My heart slams against my ribs, sending shockwaves of surprise through me. I know he can feel it too, for a pale shimmer of worry flows from him. I try to smile, try to reassure him, but even that feels like too much of an effort. I swallow and find my throat dry.

"Water," I croak, then swallow again.

He's still in me and when he makes to move, I find myself gripping his shoulders. Fear twists my heart. I am sure if I let him go, I'll never find him again. I can't let him go.

Not yet.

Not ever.

He raises his chest, his skin reluctantly parting from mine. The cool air rushing in between us makes me shiver. If he leaves now, I'll come to my senses. I'd have to think, and figure out my unusual response to him. I'm not ready yet for that rational part of me to kick in.

Instead, I pull him closer. My nails dig into his shoulders.

"Don't go," I say, my voice whispers over his skin.

Confusion flickers over his face. He senses my emotions twisting inside. Knows that if he leaves now, things will change and he's not ready for that, either.

Pushing aside everything else from my mind, I raise my head and sink my teeth into his lower lip.

We make love again.

A FEW HOURS LATER, HE shakes me awake and hands me a glass of water. I gulp it down. Then, take the jug of water he's placed next to the bed, and drink most of that too. Some of the water drips down my neck, onto my chest. Wiping my face, I place the jug back on the side with a thump. Look up to find his eyes on my face.

His lips curve in a smile.

I flush a little.

"Thirsty…" I say.

His eyes drop to my chest where I spilled the water and a slow burn kicks in at the base of my belly, creeping up my skin. I can't take my eyes off his face, though.

His gaze deepens, the green bleeding out, going colorless, an almost silvery shine coming into them. He leans forward, and I still can't move. My heart begins a slow thud, and I swallow as his breath flows over my skin. Flicking out his tongue, he catches a drop of water trickling down between my breasts.

A thick cloud of heat wafts off his chest and slams into me. I find myself pushing back from him. Backing away from the intent in his eyes. Yet, I'm strangely excited. A shiver of anticipation runs up my spine.

Then, he shatters me.

"Who's Teo?" he asks.

CHAPTER 16

"TEO?" MY VOICE TREMBLES.

My heart begins to beat fast and I lay back against the bed. Try to back away. But there's nowhere to go.

"You cried out his name in your sleep." His voice is mild.

"Ah!"

I must have been more tired than usual. What else had I let slip?

My eyes skitter toward the open window near the deck. The sky is still dark outside, but a faint lightening in the distance indicates dawn is not far off.

I'm avoiding the question. Mikhail notices it too, for he goes still. His muscles bunch as he folds his arms over his chest. He's still not wearing his clothes either. On his shoulder: three long scratches, the skin around them reddening.

I flush. *That has to be from me.*

I still can't meet his eyes, and know he's waiting for me to speak. He hasn't removed his eyes from my face. He's not going to move till I tell him, give him something.

Sliding past him, I wince when my skin brushes him, sending a pulse of heat through my already sensitized nerve endings. I reach for a fallen shirt – his. When my eyes swivel to him, he nods and I slide into it.

Needing to put some distance between us, I walk to the window and look out, folding my arms over my chest.

"You … love this Teo?" Mikhail asks, voice stripped of all emotion.

He tries to hide the intensity of his question, but I hear it. Know my answer is very important.

Choosing my words with care, I say my voice soft, "Teo was the kindest, gentlest soul I knew. He gave me a home, a place to stay when I had none."

"Was?" he asks.

"He's dead. The vampires turned him. Forced me to…kill him." My breath hitches. I cried over Teo, over what I'd been forced to do. There are no more tears left now.

Pushing back the emotions threatening to spill over again, I go on: "They wanted his essence. The vampires look for those who are pure. Those who can feel, and give and love." My voice breaks a little. Gripping my forearms to stop my hands from trembling, I say, "It's also why they took the orphans. Innocence, that's what they look for."

Thinking about them makes fear pulse through me again. Once again, I feel helpless. "I… We must save the orphans before the vampires hurt them."

I can feel his mind racing, making the connections, piecing it together.

"The vampires need emotional energy to survive," he says, his voice thoughtful. "Something they don't have. Vampires are ruled by the left brain. Makes them rational and cold. Too-scientific. And for them to evolve, they need emotions. Something they get only from feeding off the life force of shifters and humans who are emotional enough."

Even as he speaks, it strikes me that he's so like them. He too is driven by logic. And rational. *He's immortal.*

It helps him understand the vampires' motivations better.

But he is not them.

I'm not yet ready to know *what* he is. What other secrets is he hiding from me?

A feeling of dread runs through me as I wonder who my wolf has chosen as its mate.

Unaware of my churning emotions, he prowls toward me. My breath catches at the sheer beauty of him. He's all mahogany and ivory, and my beast wants to rub up against him.

"Shifters are primarily right brained," he says, continuing the conversation, but I'm barely listening.

My wolf basks in the heat radiating off him.

The moonlight pours over his face, casting his shoulders in shadow. I make out the planes of his sculpted chest, his concave stomach. Lower still where his desire throbs. He's aroused, and ready. And yet, that logical mind of his can't stop functioning.

"They are ruled by creativity," he says, his voice catching on the last word.

His voice glides over me again, like the rich aged whiskey he'd been drinking earlier, and all thoughts go out my head.

"Emotions make shifters highly strung." His voice deepens with desire. Is it even possible for someone to make love to you with words?

"That's why most artists and entertainers in this city are shifters."

His voice cracks. His chest rises-falls-rises, his breathing erratic.

My senses, already open, reach out to him, and when the violet and green flow over me, I gasp.

There it is again, the bond that ties us. It's stronger, drumming with energy now, feeding on the energy that swirls around us when we are together. The bond is strong enough so I can feel him through it. Feel his heat and desire and a yearning so deep it makes me shudder.

Loneliness too.

For he's been waiting. All these years, he's been waiting for me. The realization goes right to the core of me. It moves me and arouses me at the same time.

I see his soul laid bare and filled with such poignant wanting that I find tears in my eyes.

Hands on the window frame on either side of my head, he leans in close. His chest presses against my breasts, holding me trapped. Heat pools between my thighs.

Sweat glistens on his skin and before I can stop myself, I've leaned up and licked the drop that trickles down his throat.

He groans, the sound rumbling up through our joint skin, and an answering curl of heat tugs at my belly.

"Yes," I say, my eyes fluttering down. I try to rein in my desire.

What did I agree to?

My voice galvanizes him into action.

He sweeps me up, one hand around my waist, the other rough as he squeezes my thigh, running it down the side. I twine my legs around him, as he turns toward the bed.

CHAPTER 17

THE CONNECTION BETWEEN THEM HAD deepened in the last few hours. Mikhail can feel her more. Know her presence. Sense her moods.

And she can feel him too.

Already she knows him better than anyone else.

But that's still not enough. She wants more.

Leana is pushing him, asking for that part of him deep inside, the one he's kept hidden from the world. She wants him to share all of him, wants his trust, and he's not sure he can give her that. Not yet.

Now she stares up from the bed, her body coiled with that energy he sensed during their lovemaking.

Her hair flares around her like the petals of a sunflower.

Those amber eyes spark up at him. She moves restless under his gaze.

She leans up and brushes her lips across his. He winces from the bruise she gave him earlier, when she bit his lower lip.

She tilts her head, more wolf-like in that moment than she'll ever know.

Rising up, she fits her lips over his. Even as her hand closes over his arousal, squeezing him. Desire erupts in his belly and he thrusts against her hand.

She's bleeding light from her mouth and her fingertips into

him. Using her lips and teeth, she pulls at him, tugging him, sending a burst of liquid fire up his veins till it feels like he's come unmoored. He's unhinged in a way he can't recall ever being before.

A knot fisted tight inside breaks loose. Gone, dissolved in her light. For in giving to her, he finally finds meaning.

The feel of her is agony.

Then, he goes so hard he forgets everything else. Everything except the touch of her skin, the dip of her waist, which fits under his palm.

She breaks away, her breath gasping, chests heaving, hair disheveled. He can smell himself on her. He can smell her arousal too. The mix is potent. Deep. It drives him a little mad.

Forearms on either side of her head, the muscles bunching as he tries to keep his weight from crushing her, he reaches for her throat. For that space right at the base where it's furnace-hot and smelled of her. Of jasmine and sandalwood. Exotic. Erotic. *Like this adopted city of his.*

Mad with desire, he bites her right there and feels her heartbeat speed up.

She's woken up something in him. Something he still can't put a finger to, except that he's never felt so alive.

The world tilts in focus, one filled with colors and textures and hues he's never seen before.

He knows then things will never go back to being the way they were.

He's connected to her. He feels her in a way that he's never felt the presence of any other. Senses the bond between them.

Woman. Wolf. Whoever she is, she is his mate.

He'll never be alone again.

He's lost count of the number of times they've made love,

but he can't resist. Soon they'll be on their way. But for now, he must have her. One. Last. Time.

He covers her mouth with his, thrusting his tongue inside, letting it scrape against her teeth. A moan vibrates up, absorbed by him. He lets it rumble down his throat.

The taste of her, like fine wine and raisins, swirls over his tongue. It knocks into him, sizzling through him till he's sure he'll come right then.

She's building up too. He feels her tremble, as the makings of a climax ripple through her.

He wants to ride this one with her.

He slams into her.

Later, he'll curse himself for being so selfish, for wanting only to slake his own needs. For being so drunk on her nearness, that he didn't hear anything else. That he couldn't protect her.

CHAPTER 18

HE'S IN ME. THE FRESH snow and wood-smoke smell of him is all around me. That rough texture of his tongue on mine drives me mad and I melt into him. The colors surge through me: his green and silver mixing with my amber. Gold and green sparks over me, through me. The beginnings of a climax ripple out from my belly.

I scream. The silence, as he pulls the sound into him, is so erotic, it pushes me over the edge. It pulls me out of my body and blinds me with his essence. Mine. My desire.

I must open my eyes.

Must see him.

Those almost colorless-with-desire eyes.

In them, I see surprise and something else... a glitter of stubbornness.

He's holding back. A part of him still resists. Something inside of him still can't accept what is happening. Perhaps, neither can I.

I didn't think my first time would be with someone I'd just met.

You've known him forever.

A shiver runs down my back.

When he raises his hands toward me, I grip his wrists. My hands so small I can barely circle them with my fingers. His shoulders so wide, I feel small, fragile against him. The difference in our size turns me on. He's a solid wall of muscle: one covered in a sheen of desire. Lust pools in my center.

I want more.

Want more of him.

I urge Mikhail down. He hesitates then complies. Still inside me, he slides over, so I am above him.

He lets me take control, and that surprises me.

Shifter males never let a female lead in bed. But not Mikhail.

By giving me control of his body, he's won my trust. *I intend to use it.*

I shackle his hands down on the bed, on either side of his head. I lean down, still not breaking his gaze. The sweat glistens over his forehead, and I am close enough now to see the creases fanning out from either side of his eyes.

"Say it," I say, and my voice comes out husky.

I squeeze my muscles around him and he gasps. Sweat glistening on his forehead, he shuts his eyes.

When he opens them this time, the silver ripples through their green depths.

"No," he says through gritted teeth, and the intense pain I hear in it sends my pulse racing.

I lean closer and let my nipples graze his chest, to be rewarded by a plume of heat rising off him. Sweat sheens his skin now, and when I raise and lower myself on him, he bucks against me.

He tries to raise his hands once more. But I don't let go. Tightening my fingers around his wrists, I hold them down. Mikhail's holding back, still not giving me what I want. I pull at him through the mating bond.

"Say it," I growl. My wolf comes close to breaking the surface, and I leash it back, pull it in. Hold it.

"What?" he asks, his voice hoarse, wary.

"You know what," I gasp.

His eyes fall to my lips. And when he pulses heat inside me I almost come again.

Biting down on my lips, nails digging into his skin. I mark him. Push him one last time. "Say it, dammit." I swear aloud.

The green bleeds out of his eyes, leaving them so clear that suddenly I see him, see through him. See our futures entwined in the depth of his soul.

"Say it, Micah," I move against him. Flex my inner muscles around him. Bleeding light and longing, and this fierce need to own and be owned. I push all of it at him through the shared bond.

An indrawn breath from him. Then, "I'm yours," he whispers. "Yours." His voice is hoarse, subdued.

I don't feel triumphant, just broken. We've both crossed a line. Yet, what it means I don't know yet. Will not realize till much later.

I lean in and kiss him, lips clinging to him. Even as I hear voices in the distance.

Pushing away the intrusion, my attention comes right back to the male beneath me. Then he thrusts into me again. His tongue tangles with mine and I am lost. Till a cry in the distance cuts through the haze in my head.

Mikhail too must have heard it, for he goes still.

Another cry. Shut off abruptly.

Aki!

Aki's in trouble. My eyes fly open. Before I can react, hands grasp me, pulling me away from my mate.

CHAPTER 19

I SCREAM AS I'M DRAGGED off Mikhail.

My senses screech, refusing to untangle from him. Hard hands around my neck hurt me. They tear me off him, carrying me halfway across the room.

As my gaze moves to the sword by the window, I kick out and catch my captor in the shin.

He yells in pain, before a fist to my face has my neck snapping to the side. Pain rips through me, and I see black for a few seconds.

Screams erupt around me, followed by sounds of bodies hitting the floor.

I open my eyes to Mikhail grappling with a vampire. The vamp goes flying against the wall, plowing into it with such force it cracks.

Mikhail doesn't stop.

He slams his fist into another vampire, dropping him to the floor. He kicks the legs out from a third. Bending down, he snaps the neck of the fallen one. Then he slides aside to avoid another.

The vampire turns and dives for Mikhail who flings him aside. He throws the next over his shoulder. Without a breath, he punches the third in the face, kicking the legs out of the fourth.

I want to help him, and push, shove against the arms holding me down. Another fist, this time to my forehead, jolts red sparks through my brain. I black out for real this time.

When I come to, Mikhail is still fighting. I've never seen anything more magnificent. Or more deadly. A lethal combination of arms and legs that whirl so fast I can barely tell his body apart from the vampires.

More vampires glide in through the open door of the balcony. They fling themselves at Mikhail. One of them lands on Mikhail's chest, holding him down. Another throws himself at Mikhail's legs, pinning him to the floor.

A third picks up the fallen sword. He smashes the handle down on Mikhail's forehead. I cry out at the sound of steel against bone, as Mikhail lies there stunned.

They hold him down as another stalks in. This one is large, almost seven feet tall, shoulders so wide he blocks out the light from the open door. He's different from the other vampires. Bulkier and with none of that graceful silent way of walking so characteristic of these creatures.

I've seen him before.

It's the same vampire who almost took me down when they attacked the orphanage and killed Teo.

Rage lashes through me, driving away everything else. I bend down and bite the arm holding me captive. The vampire swears aloud and loosens his grip on me. I slam my elbows into him, and he yells. Then I am free, running toward Mikhail.

I don't care that I am naked.

That I don't have my sword.

All I can think is I am not going to let them kill Mikhail. I cannot lose my mate.

I don't care I am throwing myself at a creature almost four times by size.

I let the wolf inside lead.

I charge at the vampire and leap, only to be flung to the floor. The impact shudders through me, but I don't even pause. All I can think is getting to Micah. Back on my feet, I am about to spring again at the creature standing over the fallen Mikhail, when I'm gripped by my shoulders.

This time I am thrown against the wall. My head crashes into the hard surface, sending shivers of red and black through me, and I cry out in pain.

"Don't hurt her," cries the man who's walked in through the door.

A familiar voice.

Even through the blur of agony ripping me apart, there's no mistaking those indigo eyes.

"Rohan?" I gape.

He strides toward me. When the vampire doesn't let go, he punches the creature in the chest. I look on dazed, as Rohan shoves at the vamp till the massive creature moves aside.

Rohan is behind this?

When he reaches for me, I shrink away and his features twist with shock at the rejection.

Then he seems to pull himself together. "Don't make me do something I'll regret, Leana," he says.

The hard edge to his voice cuts through any doubts I have.

This time when he tries to grip my arm, I scream and kick out, catching him between his legs so he doubles over in agony.

Leaping over Rohan, I reach my sword, pull it out of its scabbard, and stand, legs braced, chest heaving as the sweat runs down my back.

Not Mikhail. Not him. The words race around my head. I will not lose him.

"Don't do it, Leana," Rohan gasps, his voice tight, but I'm

not seeing him. I can't take my eyes off Mikhail who groans and moves. When the brute who hit him earlier raises his sword again, I rush toward him.

Rohan says, his voice hard, "Another move and he dies."

I come up short. He means it, I'm sure. I stand there, my sword held up as the brute looks at me and bares his teeth in a grin. Below us, Mikhail groans again and it sends a pulse of such pain through me, I almost cry out in desperation.

His eyes fly open, taking in the fear on my face, before moving to Rohan.

"Is that...your cousin?" Mikhail coughs out blood.

His body shudders on that last word.

"No!" I cry out. I can't move. Fear pours through me, my throat closing in terror.

Without a second though, I reach out to Mikhail through my senses; through the mating bond we now share. I send him as much of my life force as I can, blowing light to him, willing him to live.

I barely notice when Rohan walks over to me, taking the sword from my hand. My arm drops to my side, but still can't take my eyes off Mikhail. His face is pale, body bleeding. The skin I'd caressed now crisscrossed with wounds glistening like angry kisses.

I am not even conscious of tears running down my cheeks, not till Rohan says, "You'd cry for him, cousin?"

I stand mute. Hands clenched, as Rohan walks across to the fallen body of my mate.

At a sign from Rohan, the larger vampire glides over to me. He grips my shoulders, holding his sword to my neck. It nicks my flesh, the blood running down my throat, but I don't pay attention. I can't even breathe as feeling of foreboding grips me.

My vision tunnels in, as Rohan holds up the sword. *My sword.*

His eyes narrow as his gaze sweeps down my body, then his glance darts to the bed, the unmade covers.

His jaw clenches and the blood drains from his face. He realizes exactly what Mikhail and I were up to in that bed till a few moments ago.

"You slept with him," Rohan snarls.

Indigo eyes going almost purple as his features twist with an emotion I can't quite place.

I wince at the accusation, seeing the room through his eyes. The rumpled sheets, pillows flung on the ground, the smell of sex in the air.

I'm not sure what to say.

How can I tell him that what took place between me and Mikhail was deeper than sex? Something ties us in a way I'd not thought possible.

Even as I think that, a presence brushes up against the edges of my mind. It has that familiar green, so-cool-it's-hot feel to it. Heat shivers through my nerves, coiling in my chest, and I know it's Mikhail. That he feels this bond as much as I do.

Fear and rage and sheer helplessness pours through the bond.

I know then it's real, what we have. *And now I'm going to lose him.*

Rohan kicks Mikhail viciously in the side, then in the face. I feel his pain like it is my own. Intense, it cuts through me. I am not even aware I am screaming again. Not till a hand crushes my mouth, cutting off the sound.

All I can do then is stare, the sound of my heart beating loudly in my ears.

Rohan's eyes lock on mine, a frown twisting his forehead.

"I am sorry, Leah." Rohan raises the sword.

I stand there, not understanding, refusing to believe the scene unfolding. Then my heart slams into my ribs before slowing.

Slower.

Slower, still.

Till I feel every. Individual. Beat. Vibrate through me.

I bite at the hand on my mouth, not caring when the sword at my neck cuts through my flesh. Arms like iron bands weigh me down, yet I scream and struggle. Kicking out. Not taking my eyes off Mikhail.

Something strikes my head.

The world tilts. I clutch at air and then I am falling. The last thing I remember is Rohan bringing down the sword on Mikhail.

CHAPTER 20

I AM RISING, FALLING, RISING again. The floor under me shudders. I am sure it's me trembling from the pain tearing through my head. Through every part of me…except my heart. For that's been torn out, leaving behind nothingness.

The vibrations continue unabated and I realize then it's the motor of a boat.

I open my eyes to the open sea. Grey and blue and green. Green like his eyes. Mikhail. Images of him on the floor and bleeding, of Rohan raising his sword, wash over me. I begin to struggle and find I can barely move. My arms and legs tied so tight, parts of them have gone numb. A gag over my mouth muffles my groan of pain as my head throbs in earnest, almost making me black out.

Mikhail.

Micah.

I reach out to him through my senses, only to be met with static. A dark blackness that screams with pain, and separation. And hopelessness. It brings tears to my eyes. It also makes me angry. Livid with rage.

I cannot, will not, give up, not like this.

I struggle in earnest, throwing myself against the side of the boat behind me. The sheet thrown over my naked body slips. I must have made enough noise, for a massive pair of legs come into sight. Someone bends down and stares at me. His face is wide, and ugly. It's the monster that tossed me against the wall earlier.

I refuse to blink, my eyes snapping on him. His features stretch in the semblance of a smile.

He stands up, turns his head and calls out, "Well, little human, your pet is up."

Rohan walks into view, a look of profound dislike on his face. He also has my sword slung over his back. He's dressed differently than the vampires. Still in black jeans and white shirt, unlike the vampires all dressed in black combat gear. He's trying his best to stand apart from them.

Rohan's not short—he's almost six feet himself—and while not muscular, he's not slender either. Yet, in front of the larger vampire he looks puny.

"I am not little," he says through clenched teeth.

The massive vampire only smirks and looks down at him pointedly. "From where I am, you are smaller and definitely weaker."

It's a pointed reference to his 'human' state. Rohan bares his teeth and holds up his hands, fists curled, ready to fight. The vampire simply laughs, but when Rohan smashes his fist into the other man's middle, the smirk is wiped off.

The vampire growls and raises his hand, only to be called to heel from the driver of the board. "Lay off, Korak. You know the boss doesn't want anyone messing with him."

The remark only seems to madden Rohan more. "Fight me, dammit!" he yells at the vamp.

The vampire growls, "I only fight warriors. The male you killed earlier, was a worthy opponent, but you? Daniel fights your battles."

He spits on the ground before walking away.

Rohan's face twists with anger, desperation, and something else. Raw hurt. I realize then he's not doing this willingly. He's not aligning with the vampires because he agrees with their plan to take over the city. He's doing it to get me.

But that he'd kill Mikhail…?

No!

I moan aloud, the sound muffled by my gag. Yet I'm sure he's heard it, for he turns and drops down to his knees in front of me.

He lifts me up so I am balanced against the wall.

I know my eyes must be a mix of pain and anger as I stare at him, willing him to take off my gag.

He says, "I am not sorry for taking you like this, or for killing him—"

Pain lances through me at his words.

I struggle against my bonds only to have him restrain me. He puts his hands on my shoulders. His touch on my skin sends goose bumps of disgust rippling through me.

When I try to shrink back, he grips my chin, holding my face up so I don't have a choice but to meet his eyes.

"If only I'd come before he got to you. Before you offered yourself to him," he says, his voice harsh. "For that, I'll never forgive you, Leana, for giving him what was mine."

His eyes narrow with rage and that obsessive look I'm coming to recognize as one beyond reasoning. I know then he is never going to let go of me.

Anger twists my gut and this time the wolf inside leaps forward, taking me with him. A growl vibrates up my throat. The world around me zooms in on the man in front. My claws slide out, pain shivering through nerve endings as they break through my skin. I am still in human form and yet my spirit is all wolf.

Tied as I am, I bend my neck and, pushing my thighs against the hard floor, I head butt him right in the middle.

Rohan falls back, the back of his head slamming against the floor.

I land heavily on his chest and my snapping jaws go straight for his throat when…I am thrown back. Rohan slaps me with such force that I arc through the air, hit my head on the side of the boat, and lie there stunned.

Flashes of red and white pain spark behind my closed eyelids. Before I can move, I am hauled up again by my throat. I gurgle, opening my watering eyes to find the vampire Korak is gripping me, holding me up like I weigh nothing.

His massive palm around my windpipe chokes me, cutting off my air. The world goes black around the edges. But the wolf will not back down.

With a last burst of adrenaline, I kick out, managing to catch him in the stomach. But it doesn't even shake him. It's like I've hit a solid wall of steel. It seems to anger him further though, for he raises me and holds me over the side, above the racing water so the spray from the waves drenches my legs. He's going to drop me in, I know it. For a moment, all I feel is relief.

Then, Rohan throws himself between us, slamming his fist against the hybrid's chest. By then I am losing consciousness. A ringing sound fills my ears.

CHAPTER 21

REACHING OUT WITH HIS SENSES, Mikhail encounters a floating, whooshing streak of black.

A perfect black.

The kind that is seamless. He can't tell where he begins and where the black ends. It pulls on him, drawing him out of himself.

He's hurt so bad his very essence is draining out. Leaving behind an emptiness. It makes him question why he always felt the need for more.

Why had it never been enough the past few years? Why had he allowed the greed of humans to draw him in? Had allowed their fear to overcome him, till he lost himself.

Emotions erupt inside, swirling, confusing him till his throat closes in and he gasps for air.

Yet, the darkness still rages, filling him with nothingness. A vacuum that rushes hungrily toward the light, toward the mating bond tying him to Leana. It's eager to harm her, to bleed her of her essence the way it emptied him.

Every part of him screams with pain, yet his only thought is to protect her.

Acting on reflex, before his mind is even fully conscious, Mikhail shuts down his senses against the mating bond. He slams down a barrier shutting Leana out. Before the grimy black can ooze through the connection and harm Leana.

Just. In. Time.

The dark rears back on itself, angry at being denied the chance to mark pristine territory.

It attacks him with renewed vigor, sending a surge of red and black pain, so angry his body convulses. He's almost thrown off the bed. Sweat pours down his chest and back, his eyes rolling back in his head senseless.

And below it all a void. A terrible emptiness for she is gone.

He can't sense her any more.

Can't feel the bond that ties him to Leana.

He finds himself adrift.

He'd come to depend on Leana, been connected to her. Through her, he sensed the collective soul of the world. He had finally understood why he'd washed ashore this adopted city of his.

As long as he was linked to her, he was grounded. She brought out those emotions that had stayed hidden for too long. But now she is gone, and once more he's alone.

And afraid.

Like he'd been before he became her lover.

Before he became a psychic coder.

Before he was thrown over by the shifters on the ship en route to this city. When he'd been a rebel leader in London...Images from his past flood his senses. The trauma of losing her shatters the barrier in his mind, and he recalls the life before he came here.

He realizes too that it was his ego that got in the way all these years. He thought he was different. When in reality he's like them. He *wants* to be like the humans and shifters in this city.

Aki was right; together he and Leana are the bridge between

species.

Together they can overcome the threat posed by Daniel and his vampires to this city. To the human species itself.

But now it's too late.

Leana's in danger.

That thought cuts through everything else. Terror races up his spine, forcing a path through the darkness, pushing away everything but that need to open his eyes.

"Open your eyes."

His eyelids flutter open. Harsh light slams against his pupils, searing his eyes. He groans, but no sound emerges, and that sends another jolt of alarm racing through him. His mouth is dry, so dry, his tongue sticking to the roof of his mouth. He tries to swallow, but his tongue is too swollen even for that. Sweat drips into his eyes and burning them.

He tries to move his arm to brush the sweat away and even that is too much of an effort. That only makes him panic even more.

His body feels too heavy. He's sure his blood has been pumped out and replaced by something heavier, denser. Something weighing him down, tying him so he can no longer move.

It brings back the pain. The memory of being beaten by the vampires. The agony of being wrenched from her twists through him. It feels like a part of him has been cut off. His heart slams against this chest, pulse racing. A shudder runs through him.

He's here.

Alive.

He swears to himself, and must have made some noise for a head appears in his line of sight, cutting off the light briefly.

He blinks but can't make out the features. Then, an outstretched arm with a glass of water appears.

He eyes it greedily, trying to sit up, but the effort sends a burst of pain through him, setting off his nerve ends jangling. Sweat breaks out over his skin.

"Take it easy," a low voice cautions.

A woman's voice.

She slides an arm around his shoulders, helping him up. She places the glass against his lips. He drinks from it, the water flowing down his parched throat. It's cool. Soothing. He coughs and she holds the glass away.

"Slowly," she warns.

His tongue flicks out, touching his dry, cracked lips, and he winces.

Then she places the glass back to his mouth, and when he's emptied it, sets it aside.

He leans back against the pillows with a sigh, closing his eyes.

"Better?" she asks.

He nods, wincing when even that small movement slashes pain through his nerve endings.

"At least you made it," she says, her voice soft.

For the first time, he detects a tremble in the words, a thread of worry that lingers. She has an accent. A crisp accent that curls her words like autumn leaves. Golden leaves like from the country he comes from.

A familiar accent like the one he used to have.

"You had me worried, Mikhail," she says.

When she says his name, he almost doesn't want to open his eyes, for he knows who this is. He can't believe it. Not her. Not here. Not like this. And yet, he must see for himself.

He opens his eyes to find her sitting next to him.

Outside, the sun has moved west, and he can see her face

clearly.

A frown pinching the skin between her eyes. Indigo eyes. Eyes that go violet with passion; that deepen to an impossibly dark blue when she's thinking. He knows those eyes.

Then she raises her hand to run it through her hair, the gesture so familiar that he is sure now who she is.

"Ariana?" Her name comes out on a sigh. "How'd you find me?"

His voice slurs with pain. A wave of tiredness washes over him, and his eyes flutter down again.

Her gentle touch soothes him as she leans forward to wipe off the sweat from his forehead.

"Aki," she says. "He managed to get you here before he collapsed."

"Aki's... alive?" Mikhail shudders in relief.

"He's wounded," she says. "The vampires messed him up, but he managed to get away from them before they killed him. Stubborn old man refuses to die."

Then another thought occurs to Mikhail. "And Devein?"

Silence.

"So, he didn't make it, did he?" His jaw clenches, and a feeling of loss twists his gut.

He swears inwardly, even as sadness is replaced by anger. He's going to avenge his old friend. And rescue Leana.

Leana!

He must get to her, if it's the last thing he does.

Thinking of her sends fear shooting through him. He gasps in pain and sweat beads his forehead, but he doesn't care.

The vampires have her.

Leana's cousin who let the vampires destroy the orphanage has taken the only thing that matters to him in this world.

She's alone out there, without even the mating bond linking her. She's terrified, and likely hurt. He must go to her.

Go to her.

Now.

Half-blind with terror, Mikhail shrugs off the sheets and is on his feet. The world around him tilts and he finds himself swaying, collapsing as his legs buckle under him.

When hands hold his shoulders, easing him back into bed, he resists, but his movements are already weak.

The darkness rushes up to claim him.

CHAPTER 22

I OPEN MY EYES AND see white. I continue staring until I realize it's the ceiling of a room.

Apparently the vampire hadn't thrown me overboard after all. I am back on land.

My gaze tracks to the side to where the sunshine is pouring through a window and when I try to move my head, pain slices through my neck. I moan, eyelids fluttering down.

But in that brief glance, I see the palm trees beyond the window and the white and blue of the sea in the distance.

Wherever I am, it's not far from the sea. The smell of seawater and fish floats in, and I hear seagulls screeching outside.

I take a deep breath and even that hurts my ribs.

A lot.

As awareness returns, I realize I am lying on my back. The smell of my own sweat mixes with the brine of the seawater. Every part of my throbs in pain.

Rohan must have stopped the hybrid from pouring me over the side of the boat. Rohan, who killed Mikhail.

Tears leak from below my eyes, and I don't have the strength to wipe them away.

Tentatively, I reach out with my senses through the mating bond as I had done last, reaching out, looking for Mikhail, to be met with… nothing. Silence. Complete and utter silence.

He's been yanked away. Cut off from me.

Panic slams through me. Desperate I search for him again in the yawning darkness. Look for that thread of light linking me to him.

Black.

Worse than black, a bottomless void, so silent it's worse than anything I've ever felt in my life. The complete lack of life, its absolute unmoving stillness sends fear clawing through me.

A certainty that the one thing, the only thing, that made sense in my life—this link to him—has been taken from me.

I saw Rohan raise the sword on him, and I am sure Mikhail is dead.

Even as I think that, terror spurts through me: a fiery liquid burning everything in its wake. Leaving me numb.

Then rage licks at the edges. The wolf trembles, twists with anger that makes it throw itself again-and-again at the bars I've slammed down against it. It tries to break through the cage.

I want to break through. Want to let my wolf loose, want it to be out so I can scream with it, howl. Let loose the sorrow pouring through me.

I want to rage against the world. Scream at the injustice of it all. Why even show me a glimpse of my mate, of how we feel together, only to have it all taken away from me?

I am on my feet and racing for the window, my only thought to get away from here, to find a way out of here and join Micah. I'm yanked back by a collar around my neck.

I swear aloud. They had removed the restraints around my arms and legs, only to collar me. *Like an animal.*

The pain tears through me, almost blinding me, and yet I don't care.

I don't care that my fingers are gripping the collar, trying to pull it off. Don't care that I'm hurting myself, that there's blood running down my throat. That my fingernails are torn and bleeding.

All I can think is: It's. Not. Fair.

First Teo, then Mikhail is gone. But I am still here. How can I go on, all alone? I know then I can't make it on my own.

CHAPTER 23

WHEN MIKHAIL HEARS ARIANA'S ACCENT, his past comes tumbling back.

Mikhail knows now he comes from New London, and he led a rebellion against the then-authoritarian Prime Minister of New England.

He remembers Jai on a diplomatic mission from Bombay. They had negotiated a deal for rare earth metals. Jai wanted Ariana to act as a liaison between the refugees and the Council of Bombay. He insisted that Ariana go with him.

Mikhail accompanied Ariana on the ship to Bombay. It was his luck, that the ship was attacked by shifters. They had wounded him, then thrown him overboard.

Even then, Jai had known that Ariana and Jai were meant to be together.

Just as Leana and he are fated mates.

The images rush over him, fitting together like pieces of a puzzle. Mikhail also remembers who he is.

He's not human.

He's... immortal.

Aki had been right.

"Ariana," His tongue curls around the syllables of her name, testing it. It feels familiar and yet different. Like him.

"I didn't think I'd see you again, Mikhail," she says, her voice breaking on his name. "I thought you were—"

"Dead?"

When she doesn't speak, he says, "I admit I'm surprised to find myself alive. Again. How many times can a person escape death, you think?"

He tries to chuckle, then spoils the effect by coughing as the breath catches in his throat.

She reaches out to soothe him, but Mikhail leans away. A tiny movement, but she notices it. Her forehead furrows in a frown.

Mikhail knows then, that while he loved Ariana once, they'd never been lovers. He may have loved her then, but any depth of feeling is gone. All he feels now is a faint curiosity.

Unsure what to say, he settles for: "So, Aki turns up with me and you take us in?"

He winces when a jolt of pain cuts through his side.

Her eyebrows twist in concern, and she leans forward to touch him again. Before seeming to change her mind.

She grips her hands together before thrusting them back into her lap.

"I almost didn't," she confesses. The edge of her lips tilts upwards, a bitter smile. "But I couldn't turn him away. Seeing you slumped over Aki's shoulder, and Aki himself hurt and bleeding…" She swallows. "It brought back memories. Took me right back to the Jungle and the refugee camp. If it had not been for the kindness of strangers then…"

She shudders a little. "When I saw you, I thought I'd seen a ghost. But then I knew it was you." Her voice cracks. "I couldn't turn you away."

Mikhail can only imagine how traumatic it must be to see an old friend, one she thought dead. But her reaction implies more than that. Does she still care for him? *No, that's not possible.* All those years ago, she had eyes only for Jai. She made it clear to him then that they didn't have a future together.

Oblivious to his turmoil, Ariana goes on, "I can't even begin to tell you what it means to find you alive..." She shakes her head.

Grief clouds her eyes. And below that, loneliness.

She reaches out to Mikhail, and this time he lets her touch him. She touches his cheek and *that* confuses him. What should he say?

That he's with someone else?

With Leana.

Leana!

Fear zings through his blood. Panic grips him, and he can't breathe.

He forces himself to stay calm. He's alive, isn't he? All he has to do is get back on his feet and go after her.

He tries to get up, and the burning pain lashing through his nerve endings almost makes him black out. He gasps and collapses against the sheets.

"Don't move." Her voice is harsh with concern. "You were in such bad shape, I was sure you wouldn't make it. Yet, you regain consciousness the very next day. And your wounds." Her eyes dart to his chest where the sword had sliced through him. "They're already healing."

He doesn't reply.

She wrinkles her forehead, a considering look coming into those intelligent eyes.

"On the ship from London, the shifters were after you. Now it's the vampires. Bet the humans aren't far behind." Her tone is only half-joking.

Mikhail tries to smile, but even that sends another twinge of pain through him. He settles for staying still.

When she speaks next, her voice is serious. "That hybrid ... Gabriel..." She hesitates. "He threw you. I saw you go over the ship. It's humanly impossible to have survived that fall. Yet, here you are."

She runs her gaze over his features, and her indigo eyes widen. He knows the exact moment when she realizes the only possible explanation to her questions.

"Mikhail," she whispers.

Jumping to her feet, she goes to the mirror in the corner.

Only then does Mikhail take in the space around him. Even though he's half out of his head with pain, he can't help but notice the high ceilings, the elegant lines to the furniture in the room. Or the large antique mirror she's paused in front of.

He's riveted, as she runs her fingers over her cheek, before touching the strand of grey at her temple. Her eyebrows slash down in a frown and she meets his eyes in the mirror.

"I couldn't understand why looking at you felt so wrong, and yet so right. You haven't changed one bit, Mikhail," she says, her voice sharp. "You look exactly the same as when I saw you nineteen years ago."

He doesn't have a choice. He must tell her about himself. It's the only way to explain why Ariana has aged, while Mikhail looks closer to the twenty-four years he'd been when he'd last seen her.

But Ariana beats him to it.

Turning, she walks over to stand next to the bed. "I always wondered if you were quite human, even then, Micah," she says. "All those years ago, sitting in those battle strategy meetings with you, and you had this uncanny ability to predict your opponent's moves. You were too intelligent, too intuitive to be an ordinary rebel."

"So you guessed I was different from humans?"

"You always seemed so invincible, I couldn't believe you were gone, like that." She snaps her fingers.

"Except I wasn't."

He hastens to explain, trying to draw her away from the past. From the rebel leader who'd been in love with her, to what he is now: an immortal who must save his mate.

"You survived." A jerk of her head, "And you love someone else."

CHAPTER 24

"I MISSED YOU, MICAH," ARIANA says.

Those indigo eyes, which haunted him all these years, shimmer with unshed tears.

It makes him restless, this need of hers that asks for comfort. One he cannot give her anymore.

Perhaps all that time ago, in that other life of his, he had wanted her, would have died for her—*did* die for her—but not now.

It was in trying to save her that the hybrid-shifter had hurt him and thrown him over the side of the ship into the open sea.

Now as he waits for that familiar need to arise, the one that had him reaching for her in his dreams, he knows already that the one he wants is not her.

It's Leana's amber-colored eyes that look back at him now.

It's her he reaches for when he is awake.

It's her.

Only her.

And she's in danger.

Leana.

He looks past Ariana, through the open window, his senses searching for Leana by default. Only to find…emptiness.

He starts, fear lancing through him. Before remembering that he's slammed his senses shut against the mating bond.

His heart races thinking about it.

Temporary. It's temporary.

It's only to protect Leana. Till he's sure, the darkness still lurking inside him, hunting for her, is gone.

And yet, he feels so lonely.

He'd been alone all his life.

And then he met her and the mating bond had formed. And it had felt so natural like reclaiming a missing part of him.

And now without it, *without her,* he feels broken. Hollow.

It's only till he's strong enough to search for her. But already he knows he can't live without her.

And the thought once more pushes him to rise from his bed, only to have Ariana push him back.

"Mikhail!" Her voice tight with worry, she grasps his shoulders and urges him back against the pillows.

And it's a testament of how weak he is, that even though he wants to push her hands away, to shove her concern aside, he is not able to.

Truth is, even *that* movement sends stabs of pain up his nerve endings, enough to have him biting down on his lips to prevent from gasping out again in pain. Sweat breaks out over his forehead and the world darkens at the edges.

"Leah," he whispers before the loneliness pulls him under.

WHEN HE AWAKENS NEXT THE light outside has faded. There's a floor lamp lit in the far corner. He sits up and to his relief, the room stays stable.

Shoving off the thin cotton cover, he places his feet on the ground. On shaky legs, he makes his way toward the bathroom.

By the time he returns to his bed, he is sweating from the effort of being on his feet. With the last of his energy, he falls back over the covers, his breath coming in short gasps.

"Are you okay?" Ariana walks into the room, coming to a stop near the window.

She doesn't come closer, seeming to keep her distance from him.

"Rohan's your son, isn't he?" Mikhail asks.

Somewhere in that disturbed sleep, the pieces had fallen together in his head. Besides, there is no mistaking those indigo eyes.

She nods. Her body taut, restless. Like she has too much on her mind.

"Aki told me about Rohan." She hesitates, pain twisting her features.

She folds her hand over her waist, her fingernails digging into her forearms.

"I knew he was working with the vampires but this…" Her lower lip trembles. "I didn't think my son would go this far."

Grief bleeds out of her. He wants to comfort her. What any living being would have done for another.

But he doesn't.

"Jai died and our family fell apart," she says.

She turns her back to him, looking out of the window. A light breeze blows in and ruffles her hair. Yet, when it reaches him, all it brings is the memory of another: Leana's taste, her essence merging with his.

Leana. His stomach goes cold with fear. He must regain his strength. Fast. So, he can search for her.

And then his mind registers what she said.

"Jai? Dead?"

Images of the man he met briefly cascade through his mind. The man who'd loved Ariana. Their chemistry such that no one could have mistaken their connection.

"Ari, I'm so sorry!"

She stiffens; turns so her face is in profile. He sees her throat move as she swallows.

"Jai died as he lived. Serving this city. He died by his sword."

"He was killed by his own sword?" Mikhail asks, shocked.

"He was found slashed to death on the beach, his sword stolen. The corpse of his bodyguards had been torn apart. They looked like wild animals had been at them."

"Or one very angry shifter out for revenge," Mikhail says softly before he can stop himself.

"It was a shifter who killed him, all right," she says. "Whoever did it also took his sword. Ruby's sword. The sword that had led to us meeting in the first place. The same sword tore us apart, too."

Mikhail feels the hurt in those words, and for a second his mind transports him back to a memory of the two of them talking, in another country, another city. A greener city, with a cooler climate. A way of life that used to be more graceful. He blinks and it is gone.

That was the past.

This, here, now is his future.

Leana is his future. His mate.

He's sure Ariana has seen some of his thoughts on his face. She folds her arms over her chest. Ariana stands, spine erect. The lamp throws her features in relief. There's a harshness to her that hadn't been there before. Life hasn't been easy for her. Her next words confirm it.

"I lost Jai long before he died," she says, and her voice carries no trace of bitterness. "You see, Micah, his promise to his mother tore him apart. He promised Ruby he'd protect the city she loved, a city she destroyed without meaning to. He promised to take care of the sword, the only legacy Ruby left behind for him. A promise that finally killed him."

One side of her lips turns down.

"Jai loved you," Mikhail says. "I saw it with my own eyes. He worshipped you."

She puts up her hand to silence him.

"You're right. He'd have done anything to make me happy. To keep his son safe. But the citizens depended on him too.

"Jai didn't belong only to me. He belonged to this city. To the citizens who depended on him." Her voice is sincere. "I loved him even more for that. Admired him for his courage of conviction."

Her eyes lock on his glowing violet in their depths. "But I'm not like him. I am impulsive and hot headed. Jai was far better at controlling his emotions. And I miss his steadiness every single day. Yet the demands on him meant we saw less of him, those last few years."

Her sigh mingles with the sea air. She's still grieving for the man she lost. Grieving the boy she had fallen in love with.

"He wanted to be with us, but kept getting pulled away."

"And Rohan?" Even knowing it will cause her pain, Mikhail has to ask. He must know why Rohan is helping the vampires.

She says, "My son grew up searching for his father, but always only found the Mayor of Bombay."

"Perhaps you judge Jai too harshly," Mikhail says.

In the little time he'd known Jai, he'd sensed that unshakeable core of goodness in the other man. It didn't seem likely he'd have neglected his own son, not like that.

"Rohan loved his father. When Jai was killed, Rohan blamed the city for taking his father's life. He left determined to destroy

Bombay. He didn't care about the sword being taken and neither do I." Her tone turns bitter. "We're better off without it," she says.

"That Rohan would team up with the very vampires his father tried to protect the city against...that I did not expect." Ariana runs her hands through her waist-length hair, twirling it around her fingers in a nervous gesture.

"The irony is, I am still here trying to take care of Jai's legacy. Still trying to get the vampires to the negotiating table, to mediate a peace between our species. Jai's influence is stronger than I realized." She laughs without mirth. "He coached me well. And now I must continue his dream of keeping this city on track for growth."

"Even if it means activating the Hive Net?"

Too late Mikhail realizes he's revealed that he knows about the psychic weapon.

Ariana's indigo eyes going almost black with shock. "How did you know?" she asks. Then, her features tighten. "Of course. You're the creator of the Hive Net," she says, her voice harsh. "I always marveled at the sheer genius of the designs delivered over the years. Even asked to meet you a few times. But Devein always refused to reveal who it was."

"All this time he was in touch with you and yet..." A shudder runs through Mikhail.

It was fate that he'd never met Ariana. Not till now.

Fate that the project she'd employed him for had led to his meeting Leana instead.

Fate.

She inhales in surprise. The same thoughts must have gone through her mind.

"I knew when I saw the blueprint for the Hive Net that it

could not have been designed by any ordinary intelligence. But that it was you...?" She runs her hands over her face.

Her chest heaves as she takes a deep breath.

Then walking toward the bed, she drops into the chair next to it and folds her hands in her lap. Her features are once more flat.

He realizes then how much she's changed. The Ariana he'd known would never have been able to keep her emotions in check.

"I commissioned the Hive Net to win the confidence of the Council. So they'd know I had the power to keep the shifters in check," she says.

He doesn't reply. Just studies her, the shrewd negotiator she's become.

"Having access to a psychic weapon of control, made my position within the Council much stronger. It meant I could make decisions quickly, without having to always consult them. This way I could ensure the fast economic growth of the city."

She bites her lips before continuing. "But I hadn't bargained on how clever the vampires are." Her voice sharpens with worry. "Daniel, their leader, got wind of the Hive Net. He promised if I gave him the design, he'd leave the city."

She stops, her features twisting with anger and helplessness.

"And you believed him?" he asks, incredulous. "Don't you realize there's no way he'd take the design and leave?"

Folding her arms over her chest, she leans back, and looks away.

"You gave the program to Daniel already, didn't you?" Mikhail reads the guilt on her face.

Gripping her palms together, she wrings them. "I didn't have a choice. When I refused, he attacked the orphanage as a warning. His next target was the city center. If I hadn't given him the design, he wouldn't have stopped till he'd destroyed the city. This way I've bought a little more time." Her voice stretches tight. "I did what was in everybody's best interests.

"The Council doesn't have the ability to constantly keep shifters in check. As a species, they are too emotional to obey our rules. Something critical to ensure economic progress for this city."

She speaks fast, and Mikhail wonders if she's doing it to convince herself she did the right thing.

"Besides, we are too weak to keep the vampires from taking over the city. To maintain this city's status as the shining hope of the East, we must cultivate our influence globally. For that, shifters must obey the directives laid down by the Council. If that means we use the Hive Net to link to and control their minds, why not?"

Her words are persuasive, slick. She's repeated the same words many times.

"Anyway, the Hive Net is not strong enough to take over the entire city. It can only control shifters and not humans, you know that."

"You're right," he agrees. "But in the wrong hands it can be used to cause a lot of harm."

She swears aloud. "You mean he'd find a way to use that psychic weapon to control humans too, right?"

"Don't tell me you hadn't thought of that?" he replies.

"It was a risk I had to take." The color leaches out of her skin completely, leaving only those eyes burning like violet embers. "What else could I have done?"

"What if I give you a way out?" he asks.

She frowns, not replying.

"There is a way to push back the vampires," he says. "By saving the people from them, you'd get the loyalty of the citizens. They'd listen to you then, and without you having to deploy the Hive Net."

She looks at him, taken back.

"I wouldn't have believed this from anyone else," she says. "But to you, I am willing to listen."

"Does my being immortal make that much of a difference to you?" he asks.

It sounds strange to his ears when he says it aloud.

Immortal.

He'd never given it much thought.

She meets his eyes steadily. Gone is the lust, the need he glimpsed on her face. No hesitation. Now she is the Mayor of Bombay, and she wears the title in the stern look that settles over her features.

When she speaks, her voice is clear.

"It's also because I trust you." She pauses, letting that sink in. He almost believes her, but for the glint that comes into her eyes as she says it. A 'trust me' glint that instantly makes him wary.

He's underestimated her.

Perhaps even till that second, he'd been looking for the impulsive hot-headed girl he used to know, the one who used to let her heart rule.

In its place now, a suave politician, all the more lethal for she knows how to play on other people's emotions. Perhaps because she had once been emotional too, been one of the very people she now leads, it makes her more lethal, more effective, than Jai.

Mikhail realizes then, he'll have to be careful what he shares.

She leans forward. "Tell me what you're thinking."

CHAPTER 25

Vampire.

The smell lurches me awake, that characteristic scent of dry ice mixed with something sweet. Like rotting mangoes.

Mangoes I plucked from the tree in the orphanage grounds.

Last year, the summer heat had reached a crescendo, the hottest summer since the new world began, they said. But we didn't care, me and the kids and Rohan.

That particular day, we'd been out running around in the sun, on the beach, playing in the waves. Then when we got hungry, we raided the mango tree in the backyard. Rohan had climbed the tree and shaken the branches till the mangoes had fallen to the ground. We ate them till the golden juice from the fruit flowed down our chin, down our throat.

It stuck to our hands and our clothes.

Then we got thirsty, so Rohan shimmied up the coconut tree. He'd gone all the way up to where the coconuts hung in clusters, like diamonds. He flung out his hand, reaching for them till he was half-off the tree.

I gasped in alarm, sure he was going to fall. Then, screamed when he hung off the branch with one hand.

Rohan had looked down and grinned, his face full of mischief. He'd been fooling around.

I'd been livid, fuming, as my cousin threw down the tender

coconuts for us to gather.

Sliding down the tree, he walked up to me, grinning. flew into a rage and threw myself at him. We fought that day, using all the skills we learned from Aki.

We fought with our bare hands, and for the first time since Teo died, I felt the wolf move inside, wanting to come out and play a little.

We tussled, and rolled in the sand. And he looked at me, at my T-shirt stretched across my breasts.

A strange look had come into his eyes, those indigo eyes gone violet, almost black.

"You're so beautiful when you show yourself, Leana," he said.

Those words moved me a lot, for I knew he'd seen the wolf inside me. The one I'd been hiding from the world, which only Matteo had recognized. My cousin had seen the pain I still held inside.

Then he stared at my lips, and I knew, I must stay away from him.

Even then, I saw him only as a cousin. A blood-tie. He was family, so precious I'd do anything for him, even give my life.

Take his life too if needed.

All this runs through my mind, as I smell the vampire in the room.

"I know you're awake," the vampire says. His voice is patient and I sense he's been watching me for a while.

I shudder, trying to prop myself up against the wall.

"Why are you holding me here" I snarl.

"Perhaps you should ask your cousin that?"

When I don't reply he goes on, "Let's skip the initial pleasantries shall we? You've obviously figured out I am Daniel, the vampire leader."

"What do you want?" I snap back. "I'm definitely not in the mood to solve any riddles, I assure you."

His eyebrows rise a fraction. He's surprised by my response. No doubt, he's used to humans and shifters simply giving him what he wants. But not me!

"I need your help."

"Help?" It's the last thing I expected to hear. "How can I help you?"

Daniel smiles, lips stretched in the semblance of a smile.

A smile that doesn't reach his obsidian eyes. Red-rimmed eyes so characteristic of vampires.

When Teo had been turned, I saw the same red-rimmed eyes on him. Right before he asked me to kill him.

I shiver at the memory.

"It's simple, shifter girl," he says.

"Thanks to your aunt, the Mayor of Bombay, I have the design for the Hive Net, the most powerful psychic weapon ever built. And you are going to help me magnify its power."

Aunt? He's talking about Rohan's mother, Ariana. The only blood relation, other than Rohan, I have left. The one I've never met.

"On the day of the blood moon, you must use the sword to harness the power of nature. Then use it to amplify the reach of the Hive Net. Cast the net wide over the city, so every shifter *and* human is caught in it." Daniel's words cut through me.

My mind moves into high gear as I try to piece together what he's saying.

"So their consciousness will feed into it, giving you an unending supply of emotional energy to draw from?" I ask, horrified.

He has worked it all out, a solution to the one thing vampires lack: emotions.

"And this will be used only by you?" I force myself to ask. I need to keep him speaking. It's the only way to understand the larger game plan of what the vampires are up to.

"Only me?" He chuckles. "I'm not that selfish. No, it will be a lifeline for all vampires. The emotional essences will be condensed into one common pool. And we'll only take as needed, of course."

"Of course." I echo him, almost smirking at his reasonable tone. "You'd take the very essence that makes us who we are. Why not come all out and admit you want our souls," I say, not able to keep the incredulity out of my voice.

It's insane, what he's thinking of doing. Unheard of.

And yet so simple.

And he wants to use the sword to anchor this Hive Net.

"So once the Hive Net is in place, it will feed on itself, right? You set it up and the more life forces you link to it, the stronger it gets. It's self-perpetuating." I breathe out the words, not wanting to believe it, half-horrified, half-fascinated at the audacity of his plan. The scale of it is mind boggling too, for I know he won't stop at using it to control one city.

Yet, the artist in me marvels at the largeness of the canvas he has chosen to paint on.

Perhaps some of my admiration shows through, for his eyebrows rise. He looks at me, surprise evident in his eyes. In them the knowledge that he's underestimated me. He seems taken aback that I see the scale of his imagination.

"You approve?" he asks, his voice pleasant, and instantly I shrink back against the wall.

"It's clever," I say, my voice cautious.

I have his attention and must use it. Make him confide in me.

I must appeal to his ego.

"It's the dream of every pioneer, to start a movement that gathers speed all by itself. Create a cause that captures the imagination of the people. One that gives you a reason to exist." I form the words carefully, knowing each nuance is important.

"And what is that, shifter girl? What is the reason for me to exist?" His lips pull apart in the makings of a smile.

He's enjoying the verbal sparring.

"You want to be like us," I say. "You want to live again, to laugh and cry and feel the myriad emotions that make us who we are. That make us, shifters real. You want our fallacies and our weaknesses to complete you. To fill that part of you that is wanting. Once the Hive Net is active, vampires will be balanced enough to mate with each other. To propagate a pure species."

I piece it together as I speak. And sense I am onto something. The words tumble out as the excitement of discovering his real plans has me in thrall, "You want to use me to amplify the power of the Hive Net, so it's strong enough to become a collective consciousness. A link to control every shifter and human in this city in one go.

"It was only intended for shifters, but you'll use the sword to boost its signal so it becomes strong enough to link to every human too. You want me to channel the power of the sword into the Hive Net, making it potent enough to control the entire city including the Council." I shudder as the realization sinks in.

My voice dies as I stare in shock. The look on his face tells me I'm right.

The vampire nods, his gaze thoughtful. He takes a step forward, then another, and drops to his haunches, so he's eye level with me.

He's so close now I can see the individual eyelashes, blonde and tipped with dark brown at the edges. See the fine crinkles at the edge of his eyes and the streaks of grey at the temple that only add to his handsome appearance.

Before I can react, he reaches out and captures my chin between his fingers, turning my face this way and then that.

"Your cousin was right." His voice lowers a notch. "There's more to you than meets the eye. You are more than a tempestuous shifter. Your emotions are the gateway to a complex intelligent courageous being. And a fighter too. You're an enticing package, my dear. And your contradictions just made you more valuable than your cousin or your boyfriend."

"Wha-what do you mean?" I force out the words through lips gone dry. My throat closes in as he looks at me steadily.

He finally drops his hand to his side and says, "You've made me realize I have more use for you, after all. Not only are you going to use the sword and help me amplify the Hive Net, you'll also help me continue the vampire race."

The horror of his words sink in.

Before I can stop myself, before the rational human part of me can even absorb what he is saying, the wolf is already reacting. I am up and springing on him, but he's fast.

Faster than any shifter I know.

Before I can blink, he's on the other side of the room, leaning against the wall, his arms folded over his waist as he watches the chain yank me back by the collar around my neck. I fall on my back heavily, my head hitting the floor, gasping as the pain slices through me.

"A temper, too." His tone is calm. Aggravating. "It's only going to make it all so much more interesting."

I close my eyes, curling my fingers into fists at my side. I cannot give in to him, not like this.

"What if I refuse?" I croak.

He's already shaking his head. "I don't think you under-stand," he says. "You forget I have the orphans. And one in particular, what's her name?" He snaps his fingers trying to recall. "The little girl, your favorite, isn't she?"

"Yasmin!" I gasp.

All the fight goes out of me. Rohan must have told him about Yasmin. There's no other way he knows about this too.

I am well and truly trapped.

I sit up wincing when the collar bites into my neck.

"Don't hurt her," I plead, hating myself even as I hear the hollowness in my words, but right now I don't have a choice.

"Little Yasmin will be completely safe, provided you do ex-actly as I say."

Silence.

I know he's waiting for me to speak.

Waiting for me to agree to his terms.

Waiting.

But I can't do what he wants.

I cannot let myself submit like this.

The enormity of the threat this city faces sinks in.

The balance between the species as we know it is going to change forever. And I am going to be responsible for it.

CHAPTER 26

WHEN THE DOOR OPENS NEXT, I don't bother to look up. Just lay on the floor, curved into myself.

Footsteps come close.

Pause.

It can't be the vampire. He already delivered his ultimatum.

That only leaves my cousin and I don't want to see him.

"Feeling sorry for yourself?"

I only tighten my hold around my waist.

Rohan pulls me up, propping me against the wall so I have no choice but to see him.

Taking a step back, he folds his arms over his chest.

Once more, his gaze rakes my body. Something in the way he does it, the very unfeeling, uncaring way he lets his eyes touch on my breasts, my navel, the space between my legs before swiveling back to look at my face, makes me realize this is the not the person I once knew.

It's not my cousin standing in front of me here.

He is not the man who'd looked at me with affection not that many days ago.

Gone is the carefree person who played cricket with the orphans on the beach. He even stands taller.

"Who are you?" I burst out.

Rohan's eyes widen, for it's the last thing he's expected me to say.

One side of his lips raise in a smile. "Why, cousin, you surprise me." His eyebrows twist, as he mulls something over. A confused look comes into his eyes, gone quickly.

Then he says, "Next you'll be saying you don't know me at all." His voice sounds hurt. Genuine. I know then that all this time, he had been putting on an act just for me.

All these months he pretended to be my friend, pretended to care of the orphans. All of it fake: a way to get close to me. Now he has me, at his mercy.

But I'd rather die than give in to his demands.

"You're right," I say, "I don't know you. Are you even who you say you are?"

He frowns. Dropping down to eye level says, "You hurt me, Leah—"

"Don't call me that." I bite out the words, and he slaps me.

I wince as my flesh throbs and tears prick the back of my eyes. But I don't blink, don't let him have the satisfaction of knowing he hurt me.

"You're hardly in a position to tell me what I should or shouldn't do."

I shut up.

I don't know this man at all. Why hadn't I seen the cruelty in his features? Sensed the harshness in him. The cold surrounding him, freezing him in.

He's hurting, too. The violet flickers in his eyes spark, and ebb and flow. He wants to hurt me. Rohan bends toward me, his indigo eyes fixing on mine, and for a moment, I am entranced.

In his eyes, I see a flicker of shame, gone so quickly I wonder if I imagined it. He comes closer, raising his hand, and I am sure he's going to hit me. I wince, moving back against the wall. My eyes squeeze shut and then I start for he runs his fingers through my hair.

I shudder in disgust, as his fingertips catch in the knotted coils, before he carefully pulls them free. The gentleness disguises an unleashed violence that makes me flinch.

When he buries his nose in my neck, licks me there I try to stay still, not even recoil. Not reveal the fear that jars through me. I don't want him to sense any weakness in me.

I force myself to open my eyes and look straight ahead. Pretend I am not even here in this room, with this man I'd thought of as family, trying to break me in the worst possible way.

Then he pulls back, thrusting his face at me. "You still smell of him." Rohan's voice is shrill.

Those eyes glow with anger and he grips my neck. Before I can cry out, he springs to his feet, hauling me up, till my toes are suspended above the floor. He slams me back against the wall, and I wince. I gasp as the air to my lungs dries up.

His hold on me tightens, and the world fades at the edges of my vision.

He's going to kill me.

Blind panic, self-preservation grips me, beginning to crack the walls around the wolf inside.

And yet, even now, even when I'm sure I am not going to live beyond this moment, that if I don't shift now I'll never see the wolf, *even then* I am not able to transform.

Can't shift even to save myself. Instead, the wolf trembles, burrows in deeper, blinks and waits. Waits. For what?

I let my body go limp and then I am free and falling.

Falling.

I hit the ground and lie there gasping. The breath rushes in to my lungs, the oxygen pumping through my brain, lighting up my cells.

"Fuck you, Leana," Rohan swears. The words fade in and out as I lie there, trying to come back into my body fully. "Fuck you, for who you are. For making me want to spare you, even though I want to hurt you now. I'd gladly see you die, but I can't kill you."

I can't hear him anymore. I don't understand what he's saying either. Or what he means. All I know is I am alive.

"Daniel is going to use me." I spit out the words through the ragged edges of my hurt throat. "Can't you see the vampire is manipulating you? He used your weakness to get the sword. He's going to kill you too when he gets a chance."

Rohan stiffens, and I am not sure if I got through to him. Then he turns finally and meets my eyes, and I see the confusion in them.

I push ahead, while I still have his attention. "He's going to use me to breed vampires."

"He won't." Doubt flickers across his face.

"Yes, he will." My voice cracks with pain.

Rohan swears aloud, opens his mouth to say something. Only to shut it again without speaking.

He turns to leave. "Wait," I wheeze.

Flinching when he trains those indigo eyes back on me.

I'm worried he'll change his mind and hurt me again. But I still meet his gaze, refusing to be subdued.

"The sword," I say. "What have you done with it?"

"You'll see," is all he says, before stepping over the threshold and leaving.

It's not till much later that it sinks in: Rohan spared me. He wanted to hurt me but he hadn't. He's not going to kill me. But he won't let me go either. He's going to keep me alive. Captive. Here where he has me under his control. And that only makes it all so much worse.

CHAPTER 27

THE SWEAT RUNS DOWN ROHAN'S bare chest, sinking into the soft cotton of his drawstring linen trousers. He stands on the cliff, which slopes a few feet, before dropping steeply to fallen rocks.

Waves crash over the rocks, the surf flying high in the air.

But the scene is lost on Rohan who has eyes only for the sword.

He holds the sword out, slashing it forward, then to one side, then the other, before bringing it in front of him, gripping the handle with both hands.

The blade straight in front of him, he touches his forehead, slick with sweat, to the edge. The blade is so sharp it quivers against his skin, like the pulse of a highly strung woman.

Like Leana.

Gritting his teeth, he pushes her out of his mind and refocuses on the sword.

The blade nicks his forehead, drawing blood, but he doesn't care. Eyes closed, he tries to feel the power of the sword. Tries to draw on it, to let it flow through his veins. He looks for power... but there's nothing.

He has been working out with it for days, and yet the sword feels foreign in his hands.

Is it his imagination or is something stopping him? Perhaps the blood of his ancestors is rejecting him.

The same bloodline that had marked him. Left him with that particular burden of being the son who'd never measure up to the deeds of his father or his ancestors before.

All these years, he'd never understood his father.

He couldn't grasp Jai's sense of duty which had driven him to spend so much time away from his wife and son. And when Jai died, the sense of loss had been crippling.

It had felt unreal to find his father gone.

Like he'd watched it all from far away, or perhaps he'd simply been in shock.

It had shattered his mother too.

Ariana had loved Jai, and yet in those last years of their life together, he had also seen his parents grow apart.

He'd been witness to their frequent arguments, with Ariana accusing Jai of caring more for the Council and the city than for her. The arrival of the vampires and the growing political clout of their leader Daniel Winter had certainly caused a lot more stress for Jai.

In his role as the Mayor of Bombay, Jai had to figure out very quickly how to neutralize their threat.

Jai himself had wanted to join hands with them, give them a seat at the table. He'd recognized the superior technological advances the vampires would bring with them, that their scientific intellect was superior to humans', one they could scarce compete with.

Jai had realized it was best to keep their enemies close where they could monitor their movements.

He suggested giving them a suburb of Bombay where the vampires could settle their own kind. In return, the vampires were to stay out of Bombay, away from its citizens including the Shifters. A deal that would have benefitted everyone.

But the Council had refused. They weren't going to part with any more land, not when real estate prices were soaring. They already regretted carving out Shifter Town, no way were they going to give away more space.

So, Daniel had claimed one of the outlying islands as his own. From there, he had masterminded attacks on Shifter Town. It wasn't long before the vampires became bold enough to foray into human suburbs, kidnapping the occasional human child too.

Rohan had always thought it had been a vampire who had attacked and killed Jai and stolen the sword.

Turned out the shifter half of the family did it. That part of the family his parents never spoke about.

Rohan knows Jai regretted having to kill Maya, but also that Jai would do it again to save this city.

He admires his father for having been able to do that, to act with that courage of conviction. He'd been jealous his father felt passionately enough about a cause to hold his ground that way.

The only thing Rohan feels this passionately about is Leana.

He's fixated on her.

Rohan felt this way since the first time he saw her. Even realizing she was his cousin had done nothing to change that.

He's perhaps even grateful that she makes him feel.

All these years, he's lived each day trying to find that kernel of something inside. Something to make him feel more than the vacuum he's trapped in. That feeling of indifference that has characterized so much of his life.

It's not even something he particularly blamed his parents for. They had loved him in their own way, just not enough to carve out a space for him in their lives.

It wasn't till he met Leana that he realized what was missing. He missed being with someone, so like him and yet not.

Someone he could identify with immediately. Oh, how he wants her. Enough to let the vampires into the orphanage, to give them access to Matteo the Hugging Saint, so they could take his life essence and turn him.

In a twist of fate, it's the attack on Matteo that finally made the Council reconsider negotiating with the vampires.

By then, Jai was dead and Ariana had invited Daniel to the table to negotiate.

The visit that had brought Daniel and him face to face. Rohan knew Daniel had been taken in by him from the time they'd seen each other.

All this runs through his mind. Sword still in hand, he turns to find the object of his thoughts right in front, staring at him.

The hunger in Daniel's eyes is strong enough to make him flinch.

Rohan holds his ground, though. He stands there, sword outstretched, breath coming out in short gasps from the workout.

"Where were you?" Rohan asks Daniel.

His jaw clenches on realizing, how much he sounded like a jealous lover.

It's not so much jealousy but more, Rohan getting used to Daniel's constant attention. Today is the first day since...since Rohan had moved into Daniel's home that the vampire has not been around.

The breath hitches in Rohan's throat when the vampire doesn't say a word.

Daniel watches Rohan. Those obsidian eyes deepen in color, till they are bottomless smudges of cinder.

The silence between them grows. Rohan wants to lower the sword, wants to snatch up his shirt to cover himself, but he can't move.

Instead, he stands there, letting the sun glisten off the blade, even as the sea breeze slaps his back, raising goose bumps on his skin.

Daniel closes the distance between them, till he stands right in front of Rohan. His breath whistles over Rohan's cheek. His face descends toward Rohan, who flinches but doesn't move. Rohan's eyes flutter down as he waits for the kiss.

But all he feels is a touch to his forehead.

His eyes fly open to see Daniel lick the sweat off his neck.

"You taste like chocolate topped with mint. Spicy with an edge that lingers." Daniel's voice is low, hard, with an undertone of wanting that is unmistakable.

Rohan shudders. He shouldn't be turned on by the vampire's words. Yet, he can't stop the answering tug that tightens his belly. Then all thoughts disappear from Rohan's head as Daniel grips the blade of the sword. He moves it down till the tip of the sword points to the ground.

He grips it so hard that purple-brown fluid runs down his palm, dripping, sizzling as it meets the muddy ground before disappearing.

He's hurt himself, let himself bleed to show he's alive. Also to emphasize the difference between him and Rohan.

"You discovered you were a vampire, how?" Rohan asks.

A question meant to distract Daniel. The first personal question he's asked since coming to stay with Daniel.

Rohan had walked out on his mother, giving up any claim to the Mayoral Mansion. Even then, he'd known Daniel would take him in, no questions asked.

He'd been confident enough to not wonder at the repercussion of his actions, not realizing then it would put Leana in danger.

"I was a scientist on deputation at the Trombay Nuclear Centre. I was researching the impact of radiation on genes, when the tsunami swept in. It threw me right into the heart of the radiation machine.

"I awoke naked, shivering, and with what I now recognize as psychic hunger," Daniel replies, his eyes dropping to Rohan's lips and staying there for a few seconds. "The hunger drove me through the broken streets of this city. I wasn't sure what I was searching for. Not till I came across a half-dead dead. And before I knew it, I'd sucked him off his psychic essence."

"Psychic essence?"

"Life force. The energy inside you. What differentiates living species from plants and animals." Daniel says. "Imagine my surprise when my fangs dropped for the first time," he chuckles. Anger and delight in his voice blend into a harsh sound.

"I used them to suck the essence from the next human and the one after. Become a psychic vampire. One with a perennial psychic hunger. One who feeds on sentient beings"

Daniel's voice drops to a whisper.

"You eat and drink, so you need food on a physical level too." Rohan's voice comes out husky and he clears his throat.

"I need more than that *on a physical level.*" Daniel's eyes drop to Rohan's crotch. His meaning is apparent.

"And blood?" Rohan's voice comes out jerky.

Daniel's eyes sear a path to Rohan's neck.

"A poor second choice. The life force from blood is diluted. We prefer the concentrated essence that drawn from the soul." Daniel meets Rohan's eyes.

The naked need in them sends a pulse of heat racing down Rohan's spine.

Daniel sharing his past, opening himself up this way, all of it confuses Rohan. It makes Rohan want to share more about himself too; but he stops himself. His mind races ahead trying to understand what else Daniel wants.

And it hits him then.

The vampire's going to use Leana to get what he wants. And then strip her off her life force.

Unless Rohan finds a way to get her away from Daniel.

"Do you know what it's like to find out you are almost immortal, that you will not die for a very long time?" Daniel laughs, the sound strangely broken.

"So, you can't be killed, either."

"Oh, I can." He smiles, and his eyes drop to the sword still clasped in Rohan's hand. "I can be decapitated, of course. Or ..."

Daniel's voice trails off. Then he lifts Rohan's hand with the sword, takes a step back, and places the sword against his neck. "Is that what you want?" he asks. "To kill me?"

Daniel's playing a dangerous game with him, and Rohan's not quite sure what to make of it. All Rohan has to do is plunge in the sword, sever his neck, but Daniel will not let that happen.

He's seen the vampire move enough times to know he can turn the sword on Rohan before Rohan can even breathe.

So Rohan stays where he is: at Daniel's mercy, even though it is he who holds the sword.

And all along, Rohan wonders how to get Leana away from Daniel.

Rohan knows what to do.

He must use Daniel's weakness.

Rohan must use himself. Must use the effect he has on the vampire for his own means.

As he's thinking it, he's already made up his mind. Pulling the sword back, he lets it drop.

Leaning in, Rohan thrusts his groin against the other male.

A gasp escapes Daniel's lips and before the vampire can close his mouth, Rohan places his lips there.

CHAPTER 28

DANIEL CAN'T BREATHE, CAN'T THINK. All he can taste is the dark honey of Rohan's mouth. And that's all it takes to set him on fire. He moves in, close enough for Rohan to feel the strength of Daniel's arousal, close enough to slant his lips across Rohan's mouth and deepen the kiss.

Daniel grasps Rohan around his neck.

His fingers thrust into Rohan's hair, pulling it with a violence that makes Rohan groan, the sound swallowed by Daniel.

The vibration rolls down Daniel's neck, his chest, coiling around that darkness inside of him and shattering it a little. Suddenly, Daniel is afraid.

Afraid of what he's feeling.

Afraid this is not real.

Afraid of the emotions Rohan evokes in him.

Before he can complete the thought, the vampire has let go of Rohan.

He's not even aware he's taken a step back, not till the sea breeze sways Rohan's shoulder length hair. His chiseled features call out, begging to be touched.

Refusing to give into the impulse Daniel clenches his fists by his side.

"What do you want from me, Ro?" he asks, his voice hard.

Daniel has the satisfaction of seeing the other man flinch.

Rohan folds his hands over his chest, placing a barrier between him and the vampire.

"Leana," Rohan says. "Let her go."

Daniel's jaw clenches at the mention of the shifter female.

He almost wishes Rohan had lied to him, that Rohan had mentioned anything else except Leana's name.

"And I will. I promise she will not die," Daniel lies.

And is rewarded, when Rohan's muscles relax. A sly smile glitters in those indigo eyes.

Rohan holds up his hand and runs a finger down Daniel's throat, over his chest, toward the noticeable bulge of Daniel's trousers, stopping short of running over the apex of his throbbing desire.

Daniel takes a quick breath, holds it, before forcing himself to exhale. The tug of desire in his groin reminds him again that he may be an almost immortal vampire, but his desires are still human.

"When?" Rohan lets the words hang in the air.

Daniel smiles at his impatience.

But there's no humor in his voice when he says, "Can't wait to get your hands on her? So, is this how it's going to be? You're willing to whore yourself, to sleep with me even, to save her?"

Rohan stays silent, but his jaw hardens. Those indigo eyes narrow as he meets Daniel's gaze head on.

"Isn't that what you want?" he asks. "My body?"

Even before the words are out of his mouth, Daniel is already shaking this head.

There is no hesitation when he moves forward. Closing the gap between their bodies yet again, but this time he does not touch Rohan.

"You still don't get it, do you?" Daniel asks. "It's your soul I want. Your essence. The part of you that calls out to me even when you don't realize it. That part of you that wants to redeem me if I could give you the chance. Except you had the chance, Ro, and you lost it."

He hesitates, at a loss for words, but Rohan too steps forward.

He leans into Daniel's body, so they stand chest to chest. A balance of soft flesh and hard strength, the mix goes straight to Daniel's head. The indigo in Rohan's eyes darkens to purple-black. And the desire that bleeds from Rohan almost convinces Daniel that Rohan is sincere. *Almost.*

"Does it matter, Dan?" Rohan asks.

The use of his nickname sends a shudder through Daniel. He closes his eyes, already knowing he can't stop what is going to happen.

Rohan leans up, the muscles in his arm flexing as he winds them around Daniel. He presses his lips to the hollow of the vampire's neck.

No, it doesn't matter.

If this is the only way Daniel is going to have Rohan, then he'll take it. A part of him hates that he's reduced himself to this state, to someone who will take the dregs of desire. Take whatever is left over from Rohan's feelings for Leana.

Then he forgets everything when Rohan's hand closes over his arousal.

CHAPTER 29

Three days later

SOMETIMES YOU MEET THE LOVE *of your life… only you know it's not meant to be.*

No! I wake up gasping, my skin drenched in sweat.

For a few seconds, I was back at the orphanage. In that familiar nightmare where I was forced to kill the man I loved.

I never thought I'd meet anyone else.

Till him.

Till *Micah.*

I may have screamed his name aloud. Or perhaps I just whispered it to myself. I've been chanting his name in my head, over and over again, a lifeline to this world. To the part of me that refuses to let go. Even though I can't feel him, can't feel anything of him, I want to believe he is here on this earth.

That he's probably not far off even now.

That he probably decided he didn't want me.

Yes, that's it. He doesn't want me. He decided to let go of me. Cut me off. Cut off the bond that tied us together for those few hours. That bond forged by love, by lust, by the very fire of our souls. Twined together, forever. Ever…

No, I hadn't been mistaken.

He needs me, as I need him. As much as I need the air I breathe.

Outside my window, a pale disc hangs in the sky, reminding me it's only two more days until the blood moon. The wind rustles the palm trees, then sweeps in to touch my brow. It whispers over my face, touching my skin, the tips of my breasts, before flying back out through the window, to where he is.

He is alive.

He has to be.

I must stay sane till I find him again.

Stay alive, Leah.

It's his voice.

"Micah!"

I am on my feet and rushing to the window even before I am aware of it. I almost reach it before the chain attached to my collar jerks me back again.

Anger pulses through me.

Mikhail's dead. He has to be. He wouldn't have cut me off like this, otherwise. I would have been able to sense *something*. But there's no mistaking the voice I heard... that whisper that touched me, gone before it could even register, it was Mikhail's voice. I am sure of that.

I curse aloud and the sound brings me back into my body, makes me conscious of my surroundings.

I'm in the middle of the room, back arched, still straining at the collar. Pain radiates out from where the collar is digging into my skin.

They've left me chained here, helpless. Left me alone, except for the silent vamp who comes in twice a day with my food. And even that is left by the door. My eyes go to the last meal, which I left untouched. When did I last eat?

Two, three days ago? Maybe longer. As I think about it, I become aware of a growing hollow inside. Empty, dark. Yet beneath it all I sense rage. The spark grows, catching fire, filling me with emotions I haven't felt in a long time.

Not since I first faced Aki on the ferry I'd taken to Bombay. Aki had challenged me to a fight.

I'd lost to him, of course.

Aki took my sword.

Just like Rohan has taken it now.

Rohan took what was mine. And he helped the vampire kill Mikhail...

I am going to find a way out of here and free the orphans. I am going to kill the vamps before they kill anyone else. I will have my revenge.

And that begins with standing up for myself.

Walking to the plates of drying food, I lift one up and throw it against the metal reinforced door. The sound clangs out, but it's not loud enough. Picking up both plates of food, I throw them against the door.

Better.

I catch the first as it falls and throw it back a second time.

And a third.

I raise the plates a fourth time, and this time when I throw it, it goes through the open door, past Daniel, who side-steps it with the smooth, silent, sliding motion so characteristic of a vampire.

"You are ready to talk," he says.

"I am ready to fight," I say, noting with satisfaction that my words wipe the smirk off his face.

CHAPTER 30

I WALK INTO THE ROOM on the top floor of Daniel's bungalow. It's hard to believe I was imprisoned in a room a few floors below.

My feet clad in boots of the softest leather make no sound as I pad across the wooden floor. I'd showered and put on the clothes left for me.

I don't know whose clothes they are, but they fit. The thought of the vampire picking these clothes out for me fill me with disgust, but I push those thoughts away. For now, I must play a role, play by his rules. I must bide my time till I find the opportunity to strike, to free the orphans.

I walk past the table that makes up the left corner of the room, striding out the double doors onto the balcony. Below me, a flat piece of land juts out over the most spectacular view of the Arabian Sea.

The deck sways gently in a gust of wind. I gasp and hold onto the railing, wondering if the structure is safe, when a voice remarks, "When you move with the winds of fate, it's often easier to ride out the change."

My fingers clutch the iron railing harder. Hearing Daniel's voice makes my gut twist with anger, and fear.

To my surprise, I find my nails have slid out. They slip over the railing, making hollow tapping noises.

I can't stop staring at them.

It's a sign of an impending shift.

I haven't felt this bittersweet pain in a long time. I've forgotten how the nails rip through my flesh as they slide out. This throb of adrenaline, the burn of arousal in my belly signals I am stepping into my wolf. I haven't felt any of this in a while; not since the day I shifted when the vampires attacked my father.

Now my body signals it is ready.

Perhaps being chained like a beast, has woken up the creature inside.

Perhaps I had to be treated like an animal to behave like one? *Is this what it took to unleash my wolf?*

I growl, the sound rumbling up my throat, and I swallow it down before he can hear it.

No! I am Leana. Shifter. Woman. Both.

I am Mikhail's mate.

I am the keeper of the sword.

The one who is going to end this circle of death that the sword had unleashed on us, on this city.

The one who's going to ensure the vampires would never take my soul or that of any living creature. Ever.

I turn to face Daniel, hands loose by my side.

"Fate?" I laugh at his earlier comment. "I believe in chance and in making my own destiny."

I am echoing Mikhail, without even realizing it.

"A philosopher, too?" the vamp asks. "I had you down for a warrior and an artist, *Leana.*"

He draws out my name, saying it so it comes out almost on a sigh. It makes my skin crawl. The wolf inside me growls in warning, and I bite my lips trying to calm it down. But now that it's awakened, now that it's found itself again, it can't wait to break free.

Soon.

Soon.

"Oh, yeah?" I say, my voice light, seductive. I take a step forward, then another, so I am within touching distance of the vampire. "What do you know about me?"

He looks down at me, those strange bottomless eyes of his wearing a vacant stare that sends a chill down my back. It takes everything within me to stay as I am. I will not move. Not now. I must not let him see how much he scares me. That lack of self, that nothingness in him, hints at the horrors he has unleashed on those who have come before me.

"I know you are Maya's daughter," he says. "That the blood of Catherine of Braganza herself runs through your veins. That you can harness the energy of the sword."

He takes a step forward and it's like he's moved right into that space around me, the one I let very few into.

"You have powers, Leana," he continues, his voice grating over my nerve endings. "Powers you've not begun to tap into."

"And you are going to tell me how I will use these powers for your benefit?" I ask.

He smiles without humor. "Beautiful and fearless. No wonder Rohan is obsessed with you."

"And you aren't?" I ask, my voice snide and bored enough to pique his curiosity, to keep him talking.

He raises his eyebrow, signaling that he's read my ploy.

"Oh, but I need you most of all, more than them. I need you and it's not to do with lust or the need to mate."

I try hard not to flinch at that reference to Mikhail.

"No, my dear, I need you for something bigger. To help conceive and raise a superior hybrid. Imagine, a being more genetically enhanced than pure vampire spawn. And one carrying the bloodline of Queen Catherine of Braganza herself. The result of our union will be vampire *and* shifter, yet human enough to weld Catherine's sword. Enough to control the forces of nature." He adds, "Besides, I need you to help cast the Hive Net."

"What do you mean?" I ask, my voice hard.

"*You* must use the sword to invoke the power of nature. Only *you* can draw out its power in all the intensity needed to complete my plans."

"Rohan can harness the power of the sword too. Why not use him?" I ask.

I fling the words at him, trying to distract him, trying to buy time. Anything to keep him talking.

"But you are much stronger. Emotionally and physically, you are far superior to Rohan," he says. "The female of the species is always the more resilient. I've learned to appreciate that much.

"There's an emotional strength to you, a depth that hypnotizes. Your essence, my dear..." His voice rises as he gets more excited.

He leans in close to my neck and takes a deep breath, a gesture that makes me want to shudder, but I don't.

"Your essence is the real deal," he says. "You have a courage of conviction, a tenacity I find oddly appealing. Indeed, almost reassuring. That is why it has to be you. You, Leana, are my perfect partner in every way."

Blood thuds in my ears. My heart beats so fast I have difficulty hearing him anymore. For once, even my wolf is silent, shaken at the scale of his intentions.

All along, I knew this vampire was going to change the balance of the species, but I hadn't realized the extent his twisted mind had thought this through. I didn't realize the central role he reserved for me.

For the weapon he really wants is me.

CHAPTER 31

WHILE THE WOLF IN ME is shocked by the deviousness of Daniel's vision, the human in me appreciates how neatly it all fits together.

"When did you realize…?" I force the words out, but before I can complete my train of thought, he replies.

"Realize you were key to it all?" he says, his voice serious. "Perhaps it was Mikhail and his readiness to sacrifice himself for you."

His tone turns thoughtful, even as I clench my fists at the mention of Mikhail's name.

Implied in his words is that Mikhail is indeed dead. But I don't want to think of that. Not now. If I do, I'll lose my nerve to go through this charade and that I cannot afford.

"Or perhaps, it was when your cousin agreed to sleep with me to save your life."

He pauses, even as my heart stills before starting up again, hammering against my ribs. *Rohan… no! Why would he do that? For me?*

My emotions swirl around as he continues to speak.

"It made me wonder why you appealed across species. Not just a shifter who fights well, more than a human with an artistic flair. You were the one I'd been looking for. So, I had to have you, you see.

"In fact, I am so pleased I found you that if you do as I tell you, I'll let all of them go," he goes on.

"Including Yasmin?"

"Particularly little Yasmin, who will be returned safe and sound."

I don't believe him.

Not one bit.

It's never that simple, is it?

A sound from behind him makes us both look up.

Rohan appears at the door to the balcony, his eyebrows slashing down in a frown. His eyes flit from me to Daniel. He strides onto the deck, coming to a stop between us.

It's clear from his expression that he's overheard our conversation. He now knows Daniel's real plan.

"You promised to let her go, Dan!" he says, his voice harsh. "I gave you what you wanted, didn't I?"

For a second, I think he means my sword. And then I realize he means himself. He's talking about Daniel using Rohan, using his body, to bargain for my freedom.

How could Ro do this? Can he feel so much for me that he'd share that part of him anyone would find difficult to share?

But he did it. For me.

I don't know what it means.

No, I lie. I *do* know, but I don't want to go there. Not now. Don't want to acknowledge the depth of feeling Rohan has for me. If I do, it'll make me weak, and I can't afford that, not now.

So instead I look at Daniel, keeping my eyes off Rohan so he doesn't see how his words affect me.

"See what I mean, shifter girl?" he says. "You have the mortals *and* the immortals in thrall."

"You said you wouldn't hurt her," Rohan insists, his voice

angry.

Daniel walks over to Rohan and grips his shoulder.

A strange expression crosses the vampire's face, gone quickly but not before I grasp what it is.

Daniel's hurt that Rohan has feelings for me. The kind he'd never have for Daniel.

The vampire's in love with Rohan... He feels something for Rohan and yet the next words out of his mouth seems to imply otherwise.

"Relax, lover," he tells Rohan, and a perverse look of pleasure twists his features when the other man winces at the term of endearment. "You get to play this your way, as you asked. As long as she does exactly what I ask of her." A predatory look gleams in his eyes.

"On the night of the blood moon is when I activate the Hive Net. And she will invoke the power of the sword. She will use it to harness the power of nature of lightning. Control it to amplify the Hive Net, cast it wide. In one sweep, every single shifter and human in the city will be controlled by the net," he says. "And that is only the start."

His eyes glint cold with purpose.

"I need Leana to fight at the cages, fight like she's never done before. I need her to hold the attention of every shifter and human in this city, keep them riveted. I need her to open up their emotions and root for her."

"So they are vulnerable enough, emotionally engaged enough with the fight that when the Hive Net descends on them, they will not resist," I complete his statement.

Daniel's eyes slide over to me. "Like I said, you are clever... maybe too clever."

He mutters under his breath before turning his attention back to Rohan.

Rohan shifts his weight from one foot to the other, fists clenched at his sides. "You promised to let her go after the fight," he says. "You never mentioned her using the sword." Anger threads his voice.

"It's not that I don't appreciate what you did for me," Daniel says, his voice wry, "but you should know by now that there is no honor in me. I lost that with my humanity."

Without warning, Rohan reaches out and slaps Daniel, so hard that the blow pushes the vampire back a few steps.

A stunned look crosses the vampire's face, before his jaw hardens. Then his eyes narrow, gleaming with anger. A slash of pure lust makes the red rim around those pupils flare up.

He moves fast, graceful, his feet almost not touching the ground. Before I can even blink he grips Rohan's shoulders, pulls him near, their face inches apart.

I am sure he's going to kiss Rohan.

Or perhaps bite him.

Daniel's chest rises and falls as he tries to bring his emotions under control.

Rohan is silent. He's confused too. It's clear he feels something for the vampire. The physical act from the night before means something to Rohan, too. It was more than an act of sacrifice, to save me from certain death.

Rohan hates himself for feeling it too.

For a second, Daniel simply stands there. Then he straightens, hands falling to his side, fists clenched.

"Never do that again," he says, his voice cold.

Turning on his heel, he walks off.

A breath I'd not been aware of holding leaves me in a rush. My muscles relax, only to stiffen when Daniel pauses at the doorway.

"If you have any last words for each other, now is the time," he throws over his shoulder, "for tomorrow we leave for the cages."

Then he's gone.

CHAPTER 32

WHEN DANIEL LEAVES, I TURN on Rohan. My cousin stands there, unable to meet my eyes.

"Say it." His voice is low, trembling. Filled with self-loathing. "I hate myself, Leah," he says. "I hate myself for what I did. For… sleeping with him."

He swears aloud, running his fingers through his hair.

"But you feel something for him, don't you?" I ask.

He starts, and those indigo eyes fix on mine. In them, shock. He clenches his fists at his side.

"What have I done?" he asks. "Daniel… the vampire… he did things to my body. He touched my soul. He made me feel the way I've never felt before." His features twist as he tries to process his emotions.

"It's okay," I say, my voice soft. "It's okay to feel… to love him," I offer, hesitant.

"I don't love him!" Rohan bursts out. "I love… you, Leah." His voice breaks.

But he doesn't love me.

He wants to control me.

He will do anything to have me.

He turns his back, moving to the edge of the balcony, and stands there, gripping the railing.

A slight sound from him, muffled.

He's crying.

I move fast and slip my arms around him. I lay my head against his back, feel the warmth of his skin through the shirt. That strange confusion I always have with him seeps through.

I care for my cousin. But it's different from what I feel for Mikhail. With Mikhail, my connection had run deeper. Even now, when I know he's dead, my senses can't stop searching for him.

But Mikhail can't die, he told you that.

He's immortal, so he said, but that didn't mean he couldn't be killed.

He's dead.

And yet, I can't let go of Mikhail.

Just thinking of him makes me hesitate.

I loosen my hands from around Rohan and make to step back. His hands slide over mine, grasping my palms. Then, he turns around and kisses me.

His nails dig into my arms. He captures my lips with a desperation hinting at his inner turmoil. He's trying to hold onto what he once was, what we once were to each other.

He wants comfort.

For a moment, I let him kiss me. I let myself feel the comfort of skin against skin. Of the brush of his hands around my waist as he pulls me close. The scent of his skin. *The scent.*

It's all wrong.

Different.

Too salty and light.

Too familiar.

Not the fresh snow and deep woodsy smell I wanted.

"No!"

I try to speak, but Rohan's mouth swallows the word.

As I resist, his arms tighten around me. He crushes me to him. His movements are desperate. He's trying to hold onto me. For this time when he lets me go, I'm not going to return.

He grips me so hard it hurts, and I cry out. Then, he thrusts his tongue into my mouth. I feel his arousal and that sends a jolt of panic through me. A part of me even wants to comfort him, to tell him I'll always be there for him. *Just not in the way he wants me to be.*

But then he pushes his leg between my thighs and I know then he's not going to let me go. Not till he's sunk himself in me and taken me. Not till he's wiped out all memory of his night with Daniel. Not till he's denied those feelings for Daniel. Till he's found himself again, through me.

I shove against him, struggle, beat my clenched fists on his back but there's no reaction. Nothing. He seems to harden even more, a groan wrenching up, rumbling up his chest. And *that* sends a jolt of pure panic through me.

I feel the blood thunder through my veins, a familiar rage rising inside. Like being aroused, but so much more.

A violet spark in my heart flickers. It zooms up my spine to the top of my crown. I gasp, and I know it's true. It's close now, my wolf. Closer to the surface than it's ever been.

The wolf is ready to be let out, and this time I almost give in, almost lift the bars, almost let it free.

Almost there.

Almost.

I bite down on Rohan's lips. He yells and lets me go.

The taste of his blood seeps into my mouth. It makes me feel sick and I spit it out, wiping my lips.

I want to run away from him, but I don't. If I do, he'll only come after me. If I do, I'd be forced to fight him and I don't want to do that. I don't want to lose him.

You've already lost him as a friend.

"What the fuck?" Rohan holds his palm to his cut lips, crimson trailing down his chin, spotting his shirt. "You bit me?" he asks, voice shocked, a look of utter surprise on his face.

I hold my palms face up, half-apologetic, and realize the irony. He'd come onto me, forced himself on me, and I'm the one apologizing.

"Stay away from me, Ro." I purposely use his nickname, hoping to get through to him, to remind him I am still his cousin. *Still family.*

"Why?" He looks at me, eyes blazing with a fury so strong it feels almost physical. "Why not me? You chose him, Leah. You pushed me into doing this."

His words send a chill through me.

"Doing what?" I ask.

He doesn't reply. The anger on his face mixes with resentment... and guilt. A feeling of dread clutches my heart. I take a step toward him and grip his shoulders, not caring that a few seconds ago, I had forced him to let me go.

"Tell me," I say, my voice urgent.

He moves back so my hands fall away. He's trying to separate himself, from what happened.

"What did you ask of Daniel?" I ask, remembering the vampire's earlier words.

He runs his hands through his hair, gripping the strands. His eyes screw shut, jaw muscles rippling as he clenches his teeth. Then he drops his hands to his side, fingers curled.

When he opens his eyes, I know he's made up his mind.

"It's me you're fighting in the ring," he says, his voice flat.

"What?" I ask, disbelieving. "This is insane. Why would you

do this?"

"Don't you see?" Rohan says. "It has to be this way. If I win the fight, I claim you."

"Claim me?" I ask. "You don't even love me. You don't want me," I say, desperation stretching my voice.

His lower lip juts out, the stubborn look I remember so well coming into his eyes.

He's not going to hear anything I say.

Whether he loves me or not is not even the point. He can't admit that he's already lost me.

"It makes no sense," I say.

But it does.

I know what he's doing.

I've always thought Rohan to be weaker than me. If he defeats me in this fight... then he'd have tamed me. Broken me. I would have no choice but to submit to him.

But he doesn't stand a chance.

I've always been stronger, faster than him.

I won't lose.

Understanding flashes across my face.

He nods. "If I win, you accept me," he says. "You'll do as I say."

"And what if it's me?" I say, my voice hard. "What if I win?"

"You won't," he replies.

He sounds so certain, my confidence stutters. How can he be so sure?

CHAPTER 33

Four days later

MIKHAIL WALKS TO THE MIRROR in his room in Ariana's house.

The reflection shows a man who in his early thirties, almost six feet five inches, taller than most humans. His broad shoulders are clad in form-fitting black, slightly snug so it stretches across his chest.

His trousers too are made of the same reinforced material, strong enough to withstand an attack from any sword. His feet are cramped in borrowed boots. The clothes belong to Jai: the combat gear he wore as Guardian of the city.

Without Ariana even mentioning it, Mikhail knows it.

But he hadn't asked and she hadn't said.

It feels odd wearing a dead man's clothes. By putting them on, things have come full circle. There's a strange sense of completion too.

After all, the female he's trying to save belongs to Jai's family.

Jai is watching over them even from his grave.

The thought sends a shiver down Mikhail's spine. He pushes it away, grateful to be back on his feet.

Almost at once, a lick of pain shudders through his nerve endings. A reminder that he's not yet fully recovered, but he dare not wait any longer.

Gripping the frame of the mirror for support, he curses his

own weakness.

"Leana."

Saying her name aloud sends fear racing through him. Sweat breaks out on his brow. The pain passes, leaving him weak, but stable.

He opens his eyes and this time, his gaze is drawn to the blue armband around his arm. Aria had insisted he wear it, so he would be clearly identified as being part of the Council's team of soldiers.

He'd agreed then. But now that the memories of that past life have come back with a vengeance, he can almost swear he saw Jai wear the same armband on that trip to London when they had first met.

He wonders then if this is her way of trying to keep the spirit of her dead husband alive. If she is trying to recreate Jai through him.

Mikhail reminds himself that Aria had insisted, of course, that her last few years with Jai had been difficult. They had cared for each other a lot, but there'd been a growing distance between them.

Yet, when he'd seen them together, their chemistry had been strong enough to set the space on fire.

In fact, he distinctly recalls the way they had trained on the ship carrying them to Bombay, and how they had eyes only for each other.

Perhaps Ariana misses Jai more than she cares to admit. Perhaps seeing Mikhail had only made it even more painful. He's sure it must have taken her right back to the time the three of them were together.

Jai had come on a diplomatic task to London when Mikhail had been the rebel leader there. He'd agreed to give the refugees from London a safe space in Bombay, but insisted Aria return with him.

For all his stiff demeanor, Jai had been crazy about her.

And Aria had loved him too.

The thought crosses his mind that perhaps the two of them had been so wrapped up in each other that they didn't have time for their son.

Aria had hinted that Jai had been too busy being the Mayor of Bombay to be a father.

But having seen the way Aria herself had slipped into that role, he wonders if she had not been as involved in matters of state as Jai had been. The Aria he knew had been sharp, witty, spontaneous.

The woman she turned into was methodical, calculating.

Perhaps along the way Aria had discovered she wanted more than being the wife of the Mayor.

And while she missed Jai, and would have given anything to see him alive, he wonders now if his death had also not provided an opportunity for Aria to fulfill her own ambitions.

All these thoughts run through his head as he stands there staring at his reflection.

A sound issues behind him and before he can turn, Ari comes up to stand next to him. She's dressed in the same combat clothes as him. She's still as delicate looking as he remembers her to be. But she's grown wiry, tougher, the muscles of her arms sculpted and hinting at regular workouts.

Noticing his look, she says, "Jai and I trained together a lot. It was one of the things we had in common: this love for a good workout. Jai was better at it, more disciplined, than me, of course."

She laughs then, a short bitter sound.

"You were good at fighting, too, as I recall."

The words are out of Mikhail's mouth even before he can help it. He regrets it almost as soon as he says it too. He doesn't want to give Ariana the wrong impression. Doesn't want her to feel that he's interested in her.

When she looks at him, she still sees the rebel leader who was in love with her. But he's no longer that person.

Mikhail takes a step away from her. Put's enough distance between them so he doesn't feel her body heat.

Her eyes narrow in the mirror.

"Surely you had more in common than only physical training," his voice is light.

But Mikhail's next words leave no doubt that he's emphasizing the time and distance now separating them. "You also had Rohan binding the two of you together, didn't you?"

Ariana stiffens. Mikhail knows then his words have found their mark.

He's almost regretful to have hurt her by reminding her of Rohan and yet, he's also glad to have distracted her, taken her mind away from what they once had.

He'd cared deeply for Aria. But at that time, she'd been in love with Jai and only seen him as a friend. Now the tables had turned. With Jai gone Aria wants more from him. But Mikhail has moved on. He's found Leana, his mate, and now there's no going back.

Ariana nods, not meeting his eyes. Her hands clutch into fists before she loosens them, so they hang by her side.

"Yes." She says. "Jai and I failed our only child. We drove him straight into the arms of the enemy. And now here I am, a widow who'll probably lose her son too before the week is out."

She speaks in monotone, her voice not quite bitter and yet

lifeless in a way that worries him more than the feelings she harbors for him.

She raises her hand before he can say anything. "We must pay for our sins in the same lifetime as humans. I can only wonder how it is for you as an immortal?"

Her words bring him up short.

"How many lifetimes of sins will you pay for in this one?" she adds.

Her voice is thoughtful, the truth in them sinking in as she speaks.

"I thought it was a blessing to not be afraid of death, but I was wrong. I am glad I am human. All I have to do is live out this one short life."

Mikhail does not wholly disagree with her.

The vampires had hurt him, leaving him as close to a death as he'd known.

The vampires have peeled back the layers he's used to hiding from the world. Exposed him for what he is:

As weak as any human.

As vulnerable as one who fears for the safety of those he loves.

Yet, the thought of his mate at the vampire's mercy had spurred him to recover fast.

With it, a realization that the emotions he'd thought of as weaknesses in humans are also their strength.

It gives them a richness to life, a depth missing from his.

Perhaps he'd have never realized this too if it were not for the vampire having almost killed him.

He meets Ariana's waiting gaze, his own steady. "I understand you are upset that I don't have the same feelings for you I once did. But you made your choice then," he says, "and mine was made for me when I met Leana."

At that, she goes pale, biting her lower lip.

Once upon a time, seeing her do that would have aroused him.

Now it only reminds him of Leana. Of how Leana's lips tasted when they had first kissed.

A jolt of fear runs through him, reminding him that even as they speak, the vampire may be hurting her.

"Leana," Ariana says. "You love her?"

"She is the beginning and end of everything for me," he says simply, his voice stark in its truth.

She closes her eyes, her throat moving as she swallows. There's no denying the conviction in his voice.

"You sound like Jai," she says. "You make me miss him so much."

Her grief reaches out to him. The need to comfort her is so strong that he doesn't even realize he's crossed the space between them.

"I am so sorry, Ariana," he says, raising his hand to touch her shoulder, but it's her turn to shrug it off.

That internal toughness that had helped her survive the Jungle is very much in evidence as she straightens her back, accepting the gesture for what it is.

"So am I," she says and before he can respond, she cuts him off with, "The Council is waiting to hear your plan. And every moment is precious. We must get to Leana before it's too late."

"And Rohan," he reminds her, wondering if she had purposely left off her son's name, if it was too painful for her to even acknowledge him now.

"And Rohan," she agrees.

Turning on her heel, she walks to the door and he follows.

But not before he's seen the hard glitter in her eyes. Is she crying for Jai? For her son? Regret for the future they'd never have now?

Or perhaps it's a sign that the disguise is back, that once more she's the Mayor of Bombay.

He'll never know.

CHAPTER 34

MIKHAIL FOLLOWS ARIANA ONTO THE quadrant outside the handsome Victorian building that is the headquarters of the Council. Untouched by the tsunami, the building stands as it was built more than 220 years ago.

The assembled group come to attention when they see her. Mikhail heads for the old man standing to one side.

He leans down, gripping Aki's shoulders.

"Get her back safely, immortal," Aki says.

"I will," Mikhail replies.

Aki looks older, his gray hair shining silver in the sunlight.

Mikhail knows Aki loves Leana like the daughter he never had. His grip tightens on Aki.

Then Aki steps back. "I'll be waiting for both of you," he says. "The fight is just beginning. We have much to accomplish."

Before Mikhail can ask what he means, Aki walks away. A limp, he hadn't earlier hampers his gait.

A touch on his shoulder as Ariana urges him forward to face the group. Mikhail gets his first look at the Mayor's personal elite guard. They are the best fighters in the land, handpicked by the Mayor herself. This is the only people she trusts to accompany them on this mission to rescue Leana and Rohan.

He senses the closeness of this team. They are a unit. They have been through conflicts together, saved each other's lives.

In their lead, a man in his late forties, dressed similar to Ariana in combat gear. His thick neck is ropy with muscles.

The man's grey eyes follow Ariana, before tracking over to Mikhail.

He lowers his eyebrows to meet over his sharply curved nose in a frown before moving back to watch Ariana, an almost predatory look on his face.

Mikhail is sure the man is angry with Ariana, before realizing the opposite is true. It comes to him in a flash that this man likes her. No, he's in love with her.

At Ariana's nod, Mikhail stands to her right.

Her gesture seems to surprise the guy, for he straightens.

Before Ariana can speak, he snarls, "So now we have to put up with this freak?"

He jerks his head at Mikhail so the light catches the glint of earrings at his ears. For a second, Mikhail has a sense of déjà vu, of being in a similar meeting with Jai and Ariana and a similar rude comment aimed at Ariana then.

He looks at Snarly Voice closely. Yeah, same guy. Older, larger, positively bursting with muscles. He's spent every single day of the last nineteen years working out.

So, Mikhail is not the only one to have survived the shifters' attack on the ship from all those years ago. *Are there others from Jai's original team who made it alive?* Before he can ask, Ariana replies to Cyrus' comment.

She eyes Cyrus down the slope of her nose and says in a bored voice, "Really, Cy? There's only one freak I see here, and it's not him."

Stunned silence, and then to Mikhail's surprise, the man booms out laughter.

Apparently, Snarly Voice has grown a sense of humor over

the years. Mikhail hopes his ability to fight has multiplied too. He's going to need all the backup he can get to defeat at the vampires.

"You are the best fighter we have, Cyrus," Ariana adds. Her eyes darting to Mikhail's face before she fixes those indigo eyes back on the other guy. "I hope we can work *together* to drive back the vampires. We need Mikhail's expertise in this and you know that." She lets the words hang in the air.

Implicit in them, a threat that Cyrus doesn't have a choice but to toe the line.

And yet hidden there is also a request: a plea.

Cyrus' face softens. He's heard it too and can't refuse.

A quick nod, then Cyrus straightens and walks to the head of the group.

Leaning back on his heels, legs apart, he asks, "So what does your freak—I mean, your new friend—have in mind?"

Mikhail is sure he lets the word 'freak' slip through, only to put Mikhail in his place.

Ariana's lips curve in a slight smile. She's noticed the thinly veiled insult too. She leans back a little and nods at Mikhail, giving him the floor.

He fixes his eyes on Cyrus, and then says, his voice casual, "How much do you know about the vampires?"

"I know enough," Cyrus snaps. "More than any tattooed coder who claims to be immortal does, at any rate."

Cyrus' words take Mikhail by surprise. His eyes flick over to Ariana, who raises her shoulders in a gesture that is half apology.

Of course she'd tell her team about his special 'abilities' and that he is an immortal, to give them a reason why she was bringing *him*, a rank outsider, into this.

Deciding he doesn't have any more time to lose in skirting

the issues, Mikhail drops any pretense of being calm. Instead, he says in a taut voice, "Forget everything you've heard, that sunlight burns them, or that they let their blood hunger drive them."

"You mean they can't be hurt by sunlight?" the other woman in the group asks.

Long hair braided down her back and standing almost as tall as Cyrus, she has broad shoulders and a full figure, the lush curves barely disguised by her fatigues. Her teak brown skin shimmers in the afternoon sun.

"That is correct," he says.

Her eyes widen.

"It is but extreme exaggeration. One the vamps have used to their benefit. They do have a heightened sensitivity to the sun." Mikhail says. "It causes an uncomfortable burn, almost like what a normal person feels when they have sunburn. And their eyes can burn if they spend too much time out in the sun. But all they have to do is absorb a shifter or human's life essence to counter the effects of sunshine."

"Wait." Ariana holds up her hand, her brow furrowed. "And you know all this, how?"

One side of Mikhail's lips lift in an arrogant smile. For a second, he's once again the reclusive coder, one who knows he is far more intelligent than those around him.

Then that is gone.

The one who emerged from the shadow of his past, who was charismatic, a born leader, who knew how to wheedle governments to give him what he wanted reasserts himself.

"I was a diligent student, nerdy," he replies, half-smiling at the memory. "What's important is that I know the vampires' strengths and weaknesses. And we must use this knowledge to defeat them."

He's back to being the rebel leader he was.

Back to planning how to rescue Leana.

"So, they *do* need blood?" a younger man, hair worn long to his shoulders, cuts in.

"That's your intelligent question?" The woman with the lush curves snickers, only to have him turn on her, blue eyes flashing.

Before he can speak, Ariana snaps, "Tara, Jacob, stop behaving like the adolescents you still clearly are. Don't make me regret promoting you to my elite team."

"Sorry, Ma'am… I mean, Ariana." Jacob's Adam's apple moves as he all but stands to attention.

Tara opens her mouth to say something. Only to shut up at Ariana's fierce glance.

Arms akimbo, legs spread apart slightly to balance his weight, Mikhail addresses them.

"Forget everything you ever heard about them, except for this." Holding up two fingers, he counts them off. "One, these are psychic vampires. They feed on psychic essence: the life force that makes sentient beings what they are. Feeding on blood is a poor second. They resort to it only if the psychic essence is tainted and *if* they are desperate.

"Sentient beings. So not just humans and shifters? They feed on other species too?"

When he nods, Ariana goes pale.

"And two, the fastest way to kill them is to decapitate them. Your guns can hurt them, but they won't die. And they heal very quickly."

"Like you?" Jacob says.

Mikhail nods. "Yes, like me."

"And you? How does one kill you?" Cyrus asks.

There's a quick indrawn breath from Ariana, but Mikhail doesn't look at her. Instead, he faces Cyrus straight on.

"Exactly like I'd kill you," he says, his voice firm, assertive. "A bullet to the heart or to the brain. Or a blade. But it won't be easy for I am stronger and faster than you. Fast enough to dodge bullets." He lets that sink in. "So, you see, you need me. I can help you defeat the vampires. Only I know how to stop them from activating the Hive Net."

"The Hive Net you designed for the Mayor?" Tara asks, her voice puzzled.

Ariana nods, "What I didn't tell you is that I invited the vampires to negotiate."

"Negotiate?" Tara asks in surprise.

"I asked them to leave the city, to not hurt humans and shifters further." She looks around the group as she speaks, making sure to make eye contact. "I asked them to leave the children alone."

Silence falls over the group. Once more, Mikhail is impressed by how much Ariana has changed. She's grown up, grown into this leadership role. She'd make a formidable friend and a dangerous enemy. Not one to be taken lightly.

"What did you negotiate with?" Cyrus' forehead is creased with confusion.

"With the design for the Hive Net," she replies, her voice low. Still, Ariana holds her head upright. "It was the only way," she tells the group. "I gave them the design and they were meant to leave the city. What I didn't realize was they had my son. And Mikhail's... mate."

She falters a little on the last word.

"You gave them the design to the Hive Net?" Cyrus explodes.

Stunned silence follows, broken only by the rustling of the

wind through the palm trees.

"That is why we must hurry. Their lives are in danger," Mikhail says, his tone urgent. "I designed the Hive Net so my life force is needed to power it. What I didn't know then is that the power of the sword could substitute my psychic energy. When I created the Hive Net, I didn't realize I was putting Leana in danger. It's why she was taken."

"So what are you going to do now?" Ariana asks.

"Now, I'd exchange my life for hers." He echoes Leana's earlier words.

The emotions shimmering between the two of them is lost on Tara. "It still doesn't explain why they took Leana and left you for dead. Unless—"

"Unless they wanted something else from her. Something even I don't have." Even as Mikhail says it, he knows it's true. A pulse of horror runs through him.

"Or perhaps it's a trap," Cyrus cuts in. "Maybe they spared you so you could bring us to them. Are you taking us all to our death, immortal?"

"That may well be so." Mikhail concedes, his tone impatient.

"It's your choice whether you come with me or not. You can stay here and let the vampires take over this city. Or you can come with me, save the Mayor's son's life, and defeat this threat."

Silence.

The team looks to Ariana who stares at Mikhail, her eyebrows twisted in confusion.

Mikhail curses inwardly. Every second increases the chance of Leana being hurt. He must convince these humans to back him up. These soldiers are all he has as a second line of defense. If he didn't make it out, they'd be able to save Leana. For that reason alone, it's important they accompany him.

"And what do you want in return?" Ariana finally asks, her voice measured.

Mikhail looks at her. "I defeat the vampires, and you let Leana take her sword and leave."

Ariana goes pale. "The sword is Jai's, his mother's last sign, what he inherited from her," she snaps.

"It belonged to Maya, and now it is Leana's," he says simply.

Ariana hesitates. Thinking it over, she says, "Jai gave his life for the sword. So did his sister *and* his mother. But the truth is, I have always hated it. It's never brought anything but bad luck on this family." She nods, and a look of relief steals over her face. "Take it," she says. "We're better off without it."

"You'd deprive your son of his birthright?" Tara asks, voice subdued.

"His life is more important than empty inheritance," Ariana replies, her face bleak.

Before she can say anything, a shout has them looking up.

Two guards in combat uniforms struggle with a newcomer.

The man is tall, broad shouldered, with dark brown hair. He's shorter than Mikhail. His turquoise blue eyes lock onto Mikhail's. His lean yet well-formed biceps flex as he grapples with the guards.

"Took me long enough to track you down, old chap," the man says, lips widening in a grin. Laughter lines radiate out from his humor-filled eyes. A face carved from dark marble. The sunlight gleams off his skin.

For a second Mikhail is sure he sees a vibrant blue light emanate from the male. Then Kris moves toward Mikhail, his gait relaxed, almost laid-back. Yet, there's a leashed predatory feel about him.

Another memory washes through Mikhail.

"Kris?"

CHAPTER 35

KRISHNA… KRIS… HE'D ALWAYS CALLED him Kris, Mikhail recalls.

Ariana motions to the guards, who step back, releasing him.

Straightening his shoulders, Kris tugs at his clothes. Brushing off the imprints from where the guards had gripped him.

So characteristic is his gesture, it sends a sharper wave of recognition through Mikhail.

Reaching Mikhail, Kris grips him by his upper arms.

"So, you remember me?" Kris asks, the relief evident in his voice. He throws his free arm around Mikhail's neck, enveloping him in a hug. "I wasn't sure if you recalled everything, and I don't mean your life in London."

Seeing Kris has sparked off an assault of memories from his past, and Mikhail struggles to deal with it. The images appear fast, so vivid, so real that he gasps out loud.

He's known Kris for a long time.

A relationship that transcends time and space.

When his memories of being a rebel leader in London had returned, he'd had an inkling there was more.

Mikhail had known already that he had a life even before London, one neither Ariana nor his rebel team had known about.

Except the details hadn't been clear.

But now, seeing Kris unlocks the remaining information. It flows through him, a streak of violet, silver, and green, all meshing into overlapping circles. The pattern ebbs, flows, throbs with the very essence of life itself.

A reminder that all living things, all humans, shifters, vampires, trees, even the fish in the sea, everything is connected to each other. A reminder of how he's connected to Kris.

He remembers then who he really is. Aki was right that he is immortal. He'd been not far off in saying Mikhail is divine.

A demi-god at any rate.

Mikhail is an Ascendant, like Kris. And they're here on a mission to help mortals. To defeat evil.

Any doubt about the prediction Aki had shared about him and Leana fades too.

In this avatar, as Mikhail, he must team up with Leana. Must save the city from the vampires.

All this goes through Mikhail's head as he looks at Kris. On his face, a stunned expression with the enormity of what he's recalled.

"Aren't you going to introduce us?"

Before Mikhail can respond, Kris turns to Ariana.

"You must be Aria," he says, his voice pleasant.

Ariana stiffens in surprise, her eyes darting to where Mikhail remains rooted to the spot. He's yet unable to form his thoughts into a coherent sentence.

Kris walks toward Ariana, arm outstretched. Only to find his path blocked by Cyrus. The muscular guy holds up a hand, and Kris stops in his tracks.

"Stay where you are," Cyrus' voice rings out.

It spurs Mikhail into action. He moves forward, past Kris, past Cyrus, back to his earlier spot next to Ariana.

"Meet Krishna ... Kris," he says. "An immortal like me. We are Ascendants. Reincarnated to help mortals defeat evil every time it reaches a crescendo."

Cyrus snorts. "There are more like you?" he asks, disbelieving.

A look from Ariana shuts him down.

But her voice is clipped, anger evident when she commands, "Explain yourself."

Kris replies, "We are avatars of the divine, incarnated in human form to eradicate evil. Our mission is to restore the balance of the species."

"So, angels?" Tara, who's made her way to the front of the group, asks.

Her voice is breathless. She can't quite believe what she is hearing.

Mikhail notices she can't take her eyes off Kris, either.

"We do share traits with angels, but we're *not* the same. We have more in common with our human cousins. And for that I am happy." Kris' eyes sharpen as his gaze sweeps over her.

Tara stares back unabashed. Something flares between them. Simmers. Tara is the first to flush and look away. Kris' features relax into their normal lines: the lurking humor back in his eyes.

He turns to Mikhail, "Well, are you going to tell them, or should I?"

All eyes swivel to Mikhail.

But it's Ariana who speaks, voice impatient. "No more secrets, Mikhail," she warns.

Mikhail nods, and once more wonders why it's so difficult for him to accept who he really is. All these years he's known it, had an inkling, the knowledge hidden somewhere inside of him.

Now he can't deny it anymore.

"Every time evil reaches its peak, when the earth's energy has been so corrupted by darkness that it affects those who exist here, then we, the Ascendants, are called upon to vanquish it," he says.

"And there are others like you?" Ariana asks.

Mikhail nods. "We take human forms, live out a normal life: well, as normal as it gets, anyway." His lips twist in the semblance of a smile. "You could say we are embedded here among the general population. We go about our normal lives, until called in for a mission."

"Mission?" she asks. "You mean like this one? To defeat the vampires?"

Kris replies, "Mikhail has been preparing for this all this life."

Mikhail jolts at that. "What do you mean?" he asks, and even as he says it, he knows the answer. His jaw clenches. "So being thrown mid-ocean by the hybrids, losing my memory, struggling to figure out who I was, meeting—" He stops, swallowing, unable to get Leana's name past his lips. Saying her name aloud will only hurt, and he can't bear it any longer.

"Meeting Leana," Kris completes his statement. "*That* was not part of the plan, though. It threw us when it happened."

"That's why you're here?" Mikhail asks.

Hearing his life laid out so neatly sends anger licking through his gut. His nerve endings protest at the heightened emotions, reminding him that he is also not completely healed.

"You can't stop me from rescuing her," Mikhail says in a low voice, fists clenched by his side.

Already Kris is shaking his head. "I didn't say that, bro," he replies, his voice warm, understanding. "We wouldn't ever do that, not where mates are involved."

"Mate?" Tara pronounces the word slowly as though it is foreign, an alien concept.

"Unlike humans, we immortals mate for life," Kris replies, his voice serious. "Though it's not always by choice. When the mating bond snaps into place, it sometimes takes us by surprise."

Their eyes hold again. No expression on Kris's face. He's only talking to a fellow soldier now. This time he's the one to look away. He gives Mikhail his full attention.

"So you know?" Mikhail says in a low voice. "I must find her, rescue her before the vampires get to her, before they use her in this plan to take over the city."

A plan he handed over to them. Another jolt of anguish runs through him, and he closes his eyes against the fear that twists his gut. He swears inwardly. Living among humans, he forgot his true purpose, why he reincarnated in the first place. He allowed himself to be drawn into the daily grind, for survival, for money; he forgot his true purpose. But meeting Leana had shaken him out of that space.

All of this crosses his mind, and perhaps some of it shows on his face too, for Kris grips his shoulder again. "You learned your lessons. It's why we reincarnate. And there is a reason you and Leana met. It was time," he says, not elaborating further.

Mikhail's jaw hardens. He wants to ask Kris what he means by that, but before he can, Cyrus interrupts them.

"So, if the fond reunion is over, perhaps you *Ascendants* can tell us what the plan is? Assuming you have one?" Cyrus' voice is half-belligerent.

He moves to position himself in front of Ariana. He's shielding her from Mikhail and Kris.

He's trying to establish that he's still in charge of his team and this mission. Mikhail on his own was threat enough, but Kris and Mikhail together seriously challenge his position as leader.

Mikhail also senses that together he and Kris are an unknown threat, one stronger than Cyrus and his entire team put together.

Sensing their combined power must surely strike at the very

reason of his existence, for his job as the Commander of the Guardians is what defines his life.

That and the fact that he's in love with Ariana, that he's loyal to her, means Mikhail must get Cyrus on his side, and fast.

Sure, he and Kris could take on an army of humans, of shifters even. But vampires? They're stronger, more powerful than his and Kris' combined abilities. They are the only species who can resist the joint might of all the Ascendants.

Mikhail needs Cyrus and Ariana and their team as fallback.

Nodding to Cyrus, Mikhail meets his gaze, palms raised to show he did not mean any threat to him.

"We need to work together, brother." He addresses Cyrus as an equal, hoping to make him feel more secure. Hoping to show that regardless of species, this was the time to stay strong, act as one, if they hoped to defeat the vampires.

There's no change in Cyrus' expression. If anything, his features close even more. Mikhail realizes then he's made a mistake. He'd probably come across as patronizing, and that had not been his intention, not at all.

He takes a step forward and holds out his hand.

"I need your help," he says simply. "I need your strength and your loyalty." He glances at Ariana, who's following the exchange unblinking, her features unreadable. "Are you with me?" he asks. This time his voice is sincere, soft even.

He lets his worry for Leana, his intense fear that she will be harmed, show on his face.

He realizes too that it's the first time he's asked anyone— certainly any human—for help. He is rewarded when Cyrus' features lighten. He nods, a quick jerk of his head, before gripping Mikhail's hand.

It's only a touch before he lets go.

Then Cyrus surprises Mikhail by saying, "We'll get her, this I promise you." He's surprised himself too by his own response.

"We must leave." Kris's voice is firm, but Mikhail senses the underlying thread of urgency.

"Leana is in trouble, that's why I sought you out. The vampire has taken her to the cages. And this is no ordinary fight either," he adds. "She is fighting her own blood. Her emotions will hold her back from winning this one. We must hurry…"

His voice fades.

For the first time since he slammed down the barrier against the mating bond to protect Leana from the darkness crawling through him, Mikhail opens his senses.

Clenching his jaw, he holds back the tendrils of darkness still lurking at the edges. Daniel reaches out to Leana…to be greeted by a surge of white fear so intense it blinds him.

He can't see anything except those amber eyes glowing like a trapped animal, can't hear anything but the pounding of her heart. He can taste her fear, the rush of adrenaline as it thunders through her veins. And he feels it then. That complete despair, a grey hopelessness he has never felt before. He knows then she has given up hope. Leana is going to die.

No!

He must reach her. He must tell her to fight.

Fight!

Mikhail knows then it is Leana's feelings he senses. She is terrified and he must go to her.

Now!

He takes off, runs past Kris, past the Mayor's soldiers.

He runs toward the one he's been searching for his entire life. He cannot, will not, lose her.

CHAPTER 36

I ENTER THE OPEN-AIR ARENA, Daniel a few feet behind. Instantly, it hits me: the heat from the packed bodies, the smell of sweat and rancid body odor, the roaring from the crowds—all of it assails me. All. At. Once.

Fear churns my gut.

Coming to an abrupt halt, I double over and am sick. Wiping my lips, I straighten and continue walking. Even as, my eyes are drawn to the small temple in the far corner. Beyond that, the grey-green line of the Arabian Sea surrounds the island.

The crowds give the temple a wide berth, standing clustered outside its perimeter.

Perhaps they sense that this is the scene where it had all started. Where Ruby had touched the sword to the altar inside and invoked the power of nature for the first time.

Do they know that today I am determined to end it?

One of us is going to die today, and it has to be me.

I will not fight Rohan.

The human in me had been forced to take Teo's life in cold blood.

Not again.

This time, I will resist fate, destiny. I will not give in to it.

Not. This. Time. The words keep repeating themselves in my head. I can't get rid of this sinking feeling that insists these are my last few steps, that this is my last trip.

No!

The voice echoes through my head. I look up then, and without realizing it, open my senses and search for him. I gasp when I am hit by the emotions raging through the crowd. Anger, fear, lust…It rushes to me, pours over me, through me. A grey-black seething mass of betrayal and hate and hurt.

Humans, shifters, vampires. They've seen all kinds of fights here, species taking on each other, killing each other. They've never seen family…cousins turn on each other, though. They want to hurt me, this crowd. They want to see me bleed. See me cry out in pain. They get off on it. I arouse them, a plaything that appeals to their baser emotions. They want my purity.

They want *me*.

I groan aloud as pain cuts through me. The psychic pain has me in thrall, rushing through my cells, my blood, binding down everything that is me. And for a few seconds, it's so overpowering, filling every living cell inside of me, that I want to die. Die right now.

Leana!

The same voice cuts through the grey and black hole I have fallen into and this time I know it's him. With effort, I raise my head and look around, scanning the crowds, but all I see is an ocean of faces. Not him though. There is no sign of Micah.

Yet, a flicker of hope, pink and blue, springs to life inside and unfurls. It trembles, and I rush to protect it. I slam down my senses, shutting out the crowd. Shutting all of them out.

All except that voice.

I hold onto that thread of life, use it to steady myself. I hold onto it and pull myself out of the darkness.

Taking a deep breath, with knees still shaky, I step through the open cage door and into the ring. I must fight.

Fight!

Rohan is already there on the other side of the cage.

Like me, he's dressed all in black. Tall, broad shoulders, those indigo eyes glinting in the hard spotlights.

I stutter, losing my nerve.

I can't move.

I am standing there in a corner of the cage, even as the crowds roar, calling for blood. Again. And again.

I am shoved from behind, and when I still don't move, someone pushes me so I fall to my knees, chest rising-falling-rising as the breath whooshes out of me.

Rohan circles me, moves in closer, and all I can do is watch him. He stops not one foot in front of me.

His legs muscles move as he drops to a crouch.

Sweat glistens on his brow and his eyebrows twist down in a frown.

"What's wrong with you?" he asks loud enough for me to hear him over the crowds.

"I can't fight you. I can't," I say.

"Goddamn you." He hisses. "This is not the time to be human. Fight me, Leana, or we both die."

I still don't react.

"I kidnapped you, Leana, held you prisoner—" He swears aloud. "—I tried to rape you, and yet you turn down the chance to get back at me?" He sounds frustrated, confused.

I hear something more in his voice. A touch of wonder?

He's on his knees, his head so close I can see the pores of his skin.

I realize then that part of me feels it's also my fault. Perhaps I had leaned on Rohan, sought his comfort more than I should have in the past.

Then I had found Mikhail, and all but thrown my feelings for him in Rohan's face.

I also realize the irrationality of my thoughts.

I am blaming myself for something that's not my fault. Mikhail is an unshakeable truth for me. Alive or dead, he's a part of me now.

And whether I'd fallen in love with Micah or not, Rohan would have done something similar. He's so fixated with me that it would have never made for a real relationship.

With Rohan, it's always been about possessing me. He wants to own me, my spirit. That's why he wants to break me.

But Micah...*he is me.*

Something inside relaxes as I think that. And I know it's true.

Then Rohan says, "You leave me no choice."

Before I can even draw a breath, he punches me in my side.

CHAPTER 37

I LIE FLAT ON MY back. The grey murky clouds swirl high in the skies above me. There are no stars tonight.

Closing my eyes, I let the tears leak through. When I open them, he's there. Mikhail.

Silver green eyes stare down at me. Almost colorless. Their coolness a mirror I want to flow into. When he holds out his hand, I take it. He pulls me to my feet, still not breaking eye contact.

The rest of the arena recedes.

I don't see Rohan standing not four feet away.

Don't see the crowds throwing themselves against the bars of the cage.

Don't hear the indrawn breath from Daniel, who stands outside the cage door.

Don't even see the sea begin to churn around the island.

All I see are his eyes. I feel the violet and green from him reach out to me, plug back into me, a deep, dense connection that once more ties us together. Feel the violet sparks inside me leap to life, shoot up my spine and up above my crown, roaring with energy. It fills me with … strength. With hope. He's alive. He really is. Then his features harden. He drops my hand.

"Fight!"

He told me once before to fight too, right here, in this arena.

Hope unfurls inside. The violet flame glows bright now, drawing on everything I was, what I always am. It burns down the barrier I had slammed around my wolf. It leaps outside, free. I am finally in my skin.

"Fight, Leana!" Micah's voice urges again, even as he moves out of the way.

A deafening roar erupts as the crowd gets on its feet.

"Fight!" The crowd screams, pushing me forward.

Yes, I must fight to save the orphans. Fight to save Yasmin. Fight with everything I have to save myself. To win this one last time.

A growl sears up through my throat, and baring my teeth, I leap.

CHAPTER 38

MIKHAIL STEPS BACK, TILL HE feels the cage bars behind him. He can't take his eyes off Leana as she leaps through the air, hands curled into fists in front of her.

Kris and Ariana and the rest—Cyrus, Tara, and even Jacob—had all come. Now they take up positions around the cage and at the exits, waiting for his signal. They planned it on the short journey to get to this island by speed-boat.

All this goes out of his head as he watches Leana move. She flings herself into the jaws of death, and there's nothing he can do.

Nothing except watch his mate tempt death again.

Fear clogging his senses, Mikhail grips the bars behind him. He wants to jump in, wants to help her, but holds himself back.

Not now. Not yet. He knows she must face Rohan herself. She must fight him, defeat him, claim the part of her still attracted to Rohan, too.

That is the only way she'll free herself.

Free the wolf inside.

Free herself to bind her spirit to his.

He watches as she slams into Rohan, taking him down. Her thighs grip him around the waist, holding him captive. She punches him to the left jaw, to the right, to his side. She slams her fists into him again and again and again, till the body under her stops moving.

The crowd goes quiet.

Sweat drips off her forehead, sparkling white in the harsh spotlights.

Chest heaving, she rises to her feet, and reels as her knees buckle under her. The fight has taken it out of her.

Her eyes find him, locking onto him. Amber clashes with silver-green.

Her features don't change, though.

She walks toward him, one step. Another. She raises her hand and reaches out to him. On her face, no surprise.

She knew he'd come.

Behind her, the figure on the ground stirs.

Mikhail's heart slams against his ribs, fear closing his throat. He moves so fast that before he's taken another breath, he has already crossed the diameter of the circular space. Mikhail leaps toward Rohan who is on his feet, his fist raised at Leana.

Landing in between them, Mikhail throws a punch so strong it arcs Rohan through the air. Rohan crashes against the bars on the other side.

He crumples to the ground, and stays still.

Already Mikhail is moving. He grabs Leana by her wrist and thrusts her behind his back. He turns, shoving his body between his mate and the vampire who has entered the cage from the other side.

And that's a mistake: turning his back on Rohan.

"Touching," Daniel says. His eyes track between the two of them, voice grim.

But Mikhail barely hears him. All he can see is the light glinting off the blade Daniel holds up.

A gasp as Leana recognizes it. It's her sword. Ruby's sword.

There's no mistaking the dull shine of the turquoise stones in the hilt.

"Don't," Mikhail says, holding up one hand.

His other grips Leana. He pulls her closer to him, moving till his body covers her, shielding shield her from the vampire.

A move not lost on Daniel.

He stays as is, watching the two of them. Daniel is waiting, Mikhail realizes. Waiting for what?

Then the muscles on Daniel's face ripple. Daniel doesn't do anything, just stays as is. Yet Mikhail knows he's up to something. He knows something is wrong. Something is going to happen, and Mikhail is going to be powerless to stop it.

Swearing aloud, he turns, but it's too late, for already Daniel is throwing the sword to Rohan.

Mikhail has underestimated him, for the human is still alive.

Gripping Ruby's sword, Rohan thrusts the blade against Leana's throat.

"Let her go or I'll kill her, right now," Rohan says, his voice cold.

CHAPTER 39

THE BLADE CUTS INTO MY throat, sending a sliver of pain shooting through me. I bite down on my lips, trying to stop myself from gasping aloud.

Yet, hearing Rohan's voice, a part of me is relieved he is still alive. That last blow from Mikhail would have felled a shifter or a vampire easily, and my cousin is *only* human. He's stronger than he seems. Humans are always more resilient than they seem.

"Move aside," Rohan tells Mikhail, his voice angry, desperate.

He's not pleased he lost to me. He'd been so sure he'd win, and then he'd claim me. Now he's been proven wrong. I'd pushed Rohan over the edge and he isn't going to accept defeat. He isn't going to let me walk away, not like this.

But he won't kill me. My cousin will not kill me.

Will he?

Sweat runs down my forehead, into my eyes, stinging them, but I don't blink. I can't take my eyes off Mikhail's face. He hasn't moved, hasn't let go of me. His arm still grips mine, tightening on it.

Fear spools out of him, bleeding out of his fingertips—and with it, a need to protect so strong it brings tears to my eyes. He'd die for me, this immortal.

Had almost died for me.

As I would for him.

Right now, he'd let himself be killed rather than see me taken again. He is not going to let me go, no way.

I know then I must live. I must find a way out of this. Must do what is needed, even if it means bending to destiny. Fate calls out to me so strongly that this time I cannot resist.

Sometimes you accept and go where you are most needed, even if it is not what you want to do.

I reach out to Mikhail then; woman, wolf, both of us, speak as one. I sense the fear. He's afraid for me. A blind panic that clogs his senses, turning that cool silver-green a churning emerald.

I say, "Let me go, baby. I promise I'll come back. I promise."

He blinks. Is it my wolf so close to the surface that gets through to him? Or perhaps it's because this is the first time I've called him that.

Despite the restive crowds, and a vampire who's ready to spring at us: despite my own fixated cousin holding a sword to me: I sense Mikhail responding to my plea.

Still, he stays as is: his muscles coiled, ready to spring.

I know what I have to do then. I let the wolf as close to the surface as I dare. Feel the pores in my body open, and the emotions pour: pinks, purples, and the blues.

For the first time since Teo, let my true desire show. Unvarnished. I show my naked self to him. Let my hunger sparkle across the space between us. Love, affection, need. For us. I show him I'm going to live, ask him to trust me. I let everything pour into that river of sensation. Let it flow over him, through him, sink into him.

The muscles of his face relax. He sees me for what I am. He nods: a slight tilt of his head. He understands.

When he steps back, I sense Rohan relax as well. He lowers

the sword, enough for me to turn.

"Take me to the temple," I tell Rohan. "That's what you want, don't you? Both of you?" I say, my eyes darting to Daniel.

The vampire is not pleased. The crimson rings around his eyeballs glow as doubt flickers across his face. Then his features resolve into a smile.

"Good to have you back, lover," Daniel tells Rohan.

This time Rohan doesn't wince at the term. He urges me to move past Mikhail. My mate watches us, eyes wary.

Out of the corner of my eyes, I notice Mikhail signal to Kris. The other Ascendant melts back into the crowd.

Still gripping Ruby's sword, Rohan makes for the exit of the cage, following Daniel walking ahead of us.

For the first time, I see Daniel's full power, for he doesn't even need to tell the crowds to part.

They seem to sense the evil in him and fall back, clearing a path for us. His team of vampires push the stragglers back.

One of them protests as we pass, "I wanted to see them rip each other apart. The first time we are getting to see human versus shifter combat, too. I want my credits back."

The male makes to push past the vampires, only to have his neck twisted. He drops to the ground.

It's a sign for the rest of the crowd to fall silent. They know something is wrong, know we are being taken to our deaths, know even that their own lives are in peril.

As I pass another shifter, he catches my eye. He raises his sleeve and shows a tattoo I recognize. A blaze of blue and black, I'd drawn it, colored it, and filled it out for him after his daughter's death. A death at the hands of these very vampires, too.

He nods, and before I can even acknowledge him, another ahead of him shows me the tattoo on his bicep, then another female turns around, raising her hair to show the tattoo at the nape of her neck.

I am not alone.

Not all in the crowd want my blood. It gives me the courage to turn to Rohan, and looking down the length of the steel sword he's holding to my neck, I ask, "Why?"

One word spoken softly, and yet I know he hears me, for his jaw hardens.

Without breaking stride, Rohan says, "I can't let you go. And if I can't have you, no one else will."

"So, you'll let Daniel suck the emotions of the shifters and humans in this city? Use it to power the Hive Net so he can track and control them?"

When he doesn't reply, I say, "And it will not stop there, you know. He's going to use the Hive Net to control other cities. He'll sell this technology to the highest bidders among governments around the world, get them to buy from him and infiltrate their cities too."

"What's wrong with that?" Rohan asks. "He offers an existence devoid of the emotions that make life so painful. If there was a way not feel, to not be torn apart by what I feel for you, I would gladly take it."

His voice is harsh, final.

I've lost him. Gone is the young man who would have done anything to save my life.

In his place stands a person whose ego won't take no for an answer. One who'd never let me go as long as he lives.

It's inevitable. I know what I have to do.

CHAPTER 40

CUTTING THROUGH THE CROWDS, WE walk past the small clearing and toward the temple. Its white dome glistens in the moonlight. As I get closer, I see intricate carvings and designs. The same geometrical shapes I'd seen around Mikhail.

It's linked. All of it. Me, the sword, this temple…and Mikhail. We're being drawn into a web that's been years in the making. My mind whirls with what it all means.

Before I can think about it further, we are already walking past the holy basil plant in the little courtyard, then up the steps leading into the inner chamber of the temple.

I hesitate at the threshold.

If I walk in, there's no going back.

The feeling of something beyond my grasp, something ominous, something I have no control over, closes in on me.

Behind us, the shifters from the crowd form a protective ring around the perimeter. They take a defensive stance against Daniel's vampires, who are falling into formation, ready to attack.

An uneasy quiet descends, broken by only the occasional low growl as a shifter threatens a vampire who comes too close.

Then Rohan pulls me with him. We step over and into the inner room.

Silence.

The noise fades away.

In here it's a different world. One with no past, no future, only the now.

It's smaller than it seemed from the outside, and the space is empty save for the small altar in the center.

Beyond it, through the small window, I see the clouds darken; they swirl around a full moon, dark, mysterious, the ivory bleeding into a coppery red. A shiver runs down my spine. My skin prickles and I am sure I've been here before.

I've seen this very scene.

Or perhaps it's the shared memories passed onto me through my bloodline.

A sound scratches behind me, and I know Daniel has followed us in.

Next to me, my cousin falters before coming to a standstill. An indrawn breath from Rohan pulls my gaze to his face. His eyes widen, and his throat muscles move as he swallows. He's taken aback, frightened by what he's seeing.

I follow his gaze. Then it's my turn to gasp aloud. The small altar glows, green and violet sparks rising from it. They shimmer in the moonlight pouring through the window. The altar senses the sword, senses us. It knows our intent.

That altar saw Ruby and Maya die, and now... *is it my turn?*

"It's time," Daniel says, but I barely hear him.

I am pushed into following Maya and Ruby, compelled to touch the sword to the altar, and call upon the power of nature to do my bidding.

A rush of adrenaline jolts me, rushes through me, filling me, expanding my cells and nerve endings. Joy, despair, happiness, all the emotions sweep through me all at once. I feel...invincible.

I know this is a trap.

I must finish the circle that started with Ruby many decades ago. And I do not know if I can.

"Rohan!" Daniel's voice cuts through my thoughts. For the first time, I sense an urgency in it.

Rohan thrusts the blade out.

His indigo eyes glow, reflecting the violet and green from the altar. He's forgotten about where we are, where he is. He didn't even particularly want to inherit the sword, and yet here he is, arm outstretched, moving toward the altar.

"Rohan, give it to her," Daniel says, his voice tight. He takes a step forward too, and I feel the anger roll off him. Black and red rage pulses from him, swirling around me, choking me, and I can barely breathe now for the evil leaking out him.

"Ro." I raise my voice, hoping to get through to him. "Rohan, give me the sword," I say, but he doesn't turn.

"Why? So you can take the one thing I can do as well as you?" His voice is childish, almost petulant. So, this is what it's been about all along? Sibling rivalry? Rohan is jealous that I am a shifter, that I am stronger. Then my choosing Mikhail over him only made it worse.

"Leana."

I turn. The object of my thoughts is outside the threshold to the temple. Mikhail is breathing hard. He must have run all the way to get here. His eyebrows slash down, lips drawn tight, hinting at the churning emotions inside.

He sets down the girl he's holding in his arms.

Yasmin.

There's a man next to him, a stranger I haven't seen before but whose facial features are as striking as Mikhail's. He pulls Yasmin to him even as Mikhail steps over the threshold.

Mikhail's eyes are steady, almost colorless. Calm. When I

open to him, waves of turquoise and blue and green flow to me. They energize me, meeting with the violet sparks that come to life inside me.

I turn to Daniel and nod. "It's time," I echo his words.

Before Daniel can react, I've leaped toward Rohan. My fist to the side of his head crumples him. I take the sword.

Then, Mikhail is next to me, grasping my arm.

Strength, a solid unshakeable feeling, bleeds into me from him. It balances me, quiets the churning emotions inside.

Together, we turn our backs on the altar and aim the sword at the vampire.

All the barriers inside me dissolve, and I let myself show. I bare myself to the world and the colors leach out of me. Purples, whites, greens and blacks, all of it flows out of me, into my fingertips and into the sword.

Next to me, Mikhail tenses as he steadies me, adding his power, his strength, his essence of oneness to mine.

We channel everything good inside us. Gather it and fling it at the vampire.

Daniel sees us move, the sword pointed at him. He reads the intent on my face.

We're going to kill him.

His eyebrows twist in surprise. He turns to run, but it's too late.

"No!" Rohan screams as he streaks past us. He throws his body in front of Daniel to shield him from the destructive power of the sword.

"Don't kill him," Rohan gasps. "I love him." The words are torn out of him. Now, when everything is about to finish, he sees a beginning for Daniel and himself.

No.

I try to pull back…when power flows into the sword.

It draws from Mikhail, from his very connection to the divine. It flows from him through the mating cord to my womb. I feel it gush up to fill my heart, overflowing down my arms, through my fingertips, and into the blade.

A jolt of fierce, unadulterated nothingness, empty and yet so full of meaning, bursts through me. For a second, I stay suspended. A lifetime.

Our combined energies flow through the sword, and out through the blade. Violet and amber and green. Sparks of gold and silver twine through the light stream. It's beautiful. It's deadly. I've never seen anything like it.

The nova of energy slams into Rohan. It goes right through him, dissolving him, before hitting Daniel. An explosion of black and red and silver crackles with electricity. The hair on my nape and forearms rises with static.

The smell of ozone and dry ice clogs the air.

Then a flare of light erupts. It's so yellow, so bright I have to shut my eyes against it.

When I come to, I'm still holding the sword, my back resting against Mikhail's chest. Both his arms are wrapped around me, his forearms resting over mine, his palms gripping my own as I grip the sword.

I look at the space where the vampire had been, the space Rohan had rushed toward, to find… nothing.

Not even so much as a mark on the floor.

They've simply…disappeared.

A shock of fear, of dread runs through me. *What have I done?* The pain in my heart is echoed by a low cry from the entrance.

I look up to see a woman standing frozen. She walks to where Rohan had last stood as he'd reached for Daniel, as he'd tried to protect his lover from the power of the sword.

She looks at me, her eyes stricken.

"My boy…" Her voice trembles.

I lower the sword to find my arms unsteady. The tremors spread through me, and my knees buckle. I'd have fallen too, except Mikhail steps even closer, supporting me. His fingers gentle, he takes the sword from me, his other arm around my waist, an iron band anchoring me. He's worried I'll be gone, as well, taken by the power of the sword.

I still don't feel anything though. I am curiously empty, spent of all emotion. I want to cry and rage at the unfairness of it all, that despite my trying my best, my cousin is now gone.

The vampire is no more, either. But I don't feel any relief at that. My mind is numb and all I can think is my confused cousin who loved me didn't deserve this.

His mother sinks to her knees at the spot.

Her lips tremble, but she doesn't cry. All along, she'd expected this to happen. Yet, she can't accept her son is gone.

"That goddamn sword," she says, her voice low, broken.

She raises her eyes to mine, her indigo eyes so filled with hate, so like Rohan's, I flinch. Then that is gone too, and there is only grief. Pain, intense pain, the kind I never want to face again, reaches out to me. It pours through me, the blacks and greys and whites, filling my eyes, so tears run down my cheeks unchecked. Inside, my wolf whimpers, and that is my undoing.

Pulling away from Mikhail, I stagger to Rohan's mother and dropping to the floor, put my arms around her, cradle her, hold her close.

"I am sorry," I say. "So sorry."

CHAPTER 41

IS IT POSSIBLE TO FEEL someone to be so much a part of you that they are in your blood, in your every pore? That they *are* you... and yet not.

After the incident at the temple, Mikhail brought Leana home, to his house, and to his relief, she let him take care of her.

Ariana had taken Yasmin under her wing. She asked Kris and Mikhail to stay on as consultants to the Council.

She had mourned her son too: her sorrow palpable in the stiff way she held herself. But that steely part of her pushed her to resume her duties in a few days. Perhaps she hoped that if she kept herself busy, she wouldn't need to think. She had thrown herself into revamping the city's security.

With Daniel's death, many vampires fled Bombay. Ariana had gone so far as to extend an invitation to the remaining vampires to stay on as legal citizens—on condition they leave the shifters and humans alone. She'd even given Daniel's bungalow, and the island it was on, to the remaining vampires, so they could set up their own township there.

The vampires had also nominated one of their own, a younger male called Ethan, as leader. He agreed to keep the peace. *For now.*

It seemed everyone had found a way to continue, everyone except Leana.

Mikhail bathed her and fed her and put her to bed that night, only to have her wake him up in the throes of a nightmare. Her guttural cries wrenched his heart and he held her sweating body as she cried. Great gulping sobs, as she tried to cleanse some of the grief inside.

She cried herself to sleep, his body wrapped around hers protectively.

Now Mikhail looks at his mate as she stares out at the setting sun. Her fragile figure barely makes a shadow as the sun's rays bathe her in reds and yellows.

She hasn't left the room in a week. Confining herself to a space from which to watch the world. The wolf inside is free, but now she doesn't know what to do with it.

If Mikhail could, he'd gladly swap her nightmares for dreamless sleep. If he could, he'd soothe the turmoil he senses inside her.

Even now, as she stands there, the air shimmers around her, hinting at the storm raging inside, tearing her apart. She blames herself for Rohan's death.

For Mikhail it feels unavoidable that Rohan met his end the way he did, for the human had made wrong choices every step of the way.

Yet, even though Leana's aware it was an accident, she hasn't stopped beating herself up about it.

"You've been avoiding me." Mikhail's voice is soft. He knows she's heard him, for her spine straightens.

She doesn't turn around, doesn't face the question in his eyes.

"He shouldn't have died, not this way." Her voice shakes with anguish. He's sure she's crying, and is frustrated that she isn't letting him see her face. Why is she refusing him this chance to comfort her?

"Rohan made a lot of mistakes. Still, why did it have to be me to kill him?" she bursts out. "Since the sword found me, it's all been building up to this. I had...*no choice.*" Her voice breaks on the last two words.

She knows there was no other way out. It was foretold that she and Mikhail would come together, that they'd use the power of the sword to overcome the threat from the vampires. Yet, she hasn't come to terms with what happened. Leana's still grieving for Rohan.

Her entire body language screams at him to leave her alone.

Is she punishing him for still being alive while her cousin is gone? Punishing him for this bond they now have, this chance at finding each other, at finding something so rare, so perfect that she almost can't believe it. Perhaps she feels she doesn't deserve it either.

She's punishing herself just as she did after Matteo's death, when she'd taken to fighting at the cages. Except this time, it's far worse. This time the wolf is out. Her emotions are all over the place, uncontrollable sensations she seems unable to make sense of.

She fought destiny with the sword, and been defeated by it. Now she's faced with another inevitable: a mating bond that formed before she realized it.

Her wolf had chosen him.

The human in her is still trying to accept him.

She wants him—that much Mikhail is sure of. Leana loves him too. She wants him as her mate. Yet, she also wants the freedom to choose. It had all happened so quickly she's still trying to make sense of it. She's thinking of leaving—

"*No!*" Mikhail doesn't realize he's said it aloud, not till she starts, and turns to face him.

The question in her eyes changes to surprise as he strides across the floor to her.

He grips her shoulders, looking into the amber eyes. Fear from her leaps out at him, and he realizes she is about to do something that will destroy them both.

"No," he says again. "Don't," he pleads, his voice anguished.

She bites her lips, looking at him, unable to speak.

But Mikhail senses the words trembling on her lips. And he doesn't want her to say it. He cannot hear what she's going to say next.

"I love you, Leana," he says, voice coming out hoarse, gritty. A stranger's voice. One filled with so much emotion he can't even recognize it as his own. "I need you. I cannot live without you. Since I saw you, it has been you. Only you."

As he says it, her eyes deepen into glowing gold. The fire in them flares to life, and the breath whooshes out of him as he realizes he's reached her.

Only you.

He repeats it, sending love, and hope, and so much else that he cannot even put words to it.

Mikhail opens himself to her.

A deep rumbling sound from her chest vibrates up, somewhere between a groan and a cry. So animalistic, and yet he's never heard anything more human.

The wolf in her had been prowling around all these days, unsure what to do with its sudden freedom. Now his touch draws it to the surface. And out. It springs free. Her nostrils flare as she tilts her head.

He sees a part of her he only felt before.

Leana rises to tiptoe. She raises her head, and fits her lips to his. His heart stutters, then stops, before erupting to life again, slamming against his ribs so hard he gasps aloud.

He hauls her against him, hauls her right off her feet so she wraps her legs around him, holding onto him.

Her jasmine and sandalwood smell pours over him and sinks into him. It goes straight to his head, making his heart flutter and then almost leap out of his chest. Mikhail is so hard, he's sure he's going to die if he doesn't have her right now.

Sweat breaks out over his forehead. He's not aware of her nails lengthening.

They dig into his back, hurting him, drawing blood. The pain mixes with the adrenaline pouring through his veins. Pleasure flares. Intense. Sends him over the edge. Drives him out of his head with wanting.

And yet, he holds back.

Muscles shudder under the force of desire leashed inside.

When he grips her waist even harder, she groans aloud.

Tearing his mouth from hers, he gasps, "Are you sure? If we do this, if we make love now, there is no going back. The bonding will be complete. If we do this, you can try to leave me but you won't be able to. Hell, you could even physically leave me but you'll never be able to get rid of me inside." He places his hand over her heart. "I'll be in you, Leah, in your head, in your very essence. Can you bear that? Can you bear being tied down to me?"

CHAPTER 42

SOMETIMES YOU HAVE TO BREAK yourself down and build it back again. Build a *you* that's so much bigger than the individual pieces.

Mikhail looks at me: human, immortal, he is both. He is mine.

The heat spools off him. It slams into me so hard that I can't breathe.

Can't think. Can't even feel.

I can't feel where I end and he begins. For he's drawing on me, pulling on something deep inside, at the very core of me. He has my wolf in thrall, has seduced the animal inside already. And now the woman in me can't resist.

Doesn't want to resist.

Is this what I was afraid of? Of immersing myself so completely in him that I lost myself?

Except, now I'll never be lost. Mikhail will find me, wherever I am.

"I'll always be there for you, Leah."

The depth of feeling in his voice brings tears to my eyes.

"Hey," he says, voice soft.

Leaning down, he licks the teardrop that has rolled down my cheek.

The feel of his tongue on my skin, the intimacy of the gesture, is both soothing and deeply arousing. He's absorbing me through his pores.

I want to surround myself with him, pour myself into him so this connection feels real. I want him.

"Take me," I say. "Show me, Micah."

At my words, his eyes dilate. The green in them lightens, leaving them colorless. I know he's aroused.

A part of me is exultant that I have this power over him. My breath hitches.

His eyes hold mine, hypnotizing. I look into those colorless pools and see through him for the first time. He's let go of even that part he hid from me earlier. He's open to me, as vulnerable as I am.

I see past him to what he is connected to.

Another pulse of heat bleeds from him, reassuring me, telling me I'll never be alone. That no matter what, I'll always have this bond to him.

He lowers me to the bed, on my back, hair splayed out behind me. When he leans back this time, I see myself reflected in his eyes for real. The desire evident in them, as he runs his eyes over my body, shocks me. I flush, heat tainting my cheeks.

My breath catches as he pulls off his shirt, the muscles rippling as he tosses it aside.

The last time we came together, in this very room, it'd been too dark to see him properly. Or perhaps I'd been too drugged by him to notice his tattoos.

The designs on his skin—the symbols scrawled across his chest and forearms—all of it turns me on even more.

The burn of jealousy takes me by surprise. That someone else touched his skin, marked him, this I cannot bear.

"The only person to tattoo you from now on is me," I say.

He raises his eyebrows, but a hint of a smile stretches his perfect lips. I know he's pleased by my possessiveness.

I see it then: the pattern in the center of his chest.

Reaching out, I trace my fingers over the hexagonal figure: two tetrahedrons, enclosed in a sphere.

There's an outer rim of six circles, then an inner rim of five, with a circle at the center. Lines extend from every circle to the center of the other eleven.

I've seen it before.

As he moves back, the light from the window pours over him, haloing him. For a second the shape pulses with a violet glow.

It's the design I'd seen around him, and one of the figures on the temple dome.

"What does it mean?" I ask, my eyes flying to his.

He says, "It's the visual expression of connection that runs through all beings. It's how I connect to the universal source of energy."

I want to ask him more, but when I see the desire flare in his eyes, I lose my train of thought. The green bleeds out of them, leaving his iris colorless.

I can see myself once more reflected in them.

The questions will have to wait for another time. Right now, I want this male. I want to lose myself in him, to forget the past and start afresh.

Heat spools off his skin, a dense cloud of want coiling around me. He pulls on me through the mating bond, sending pure desire leaping in my womb.

When I gasp, his smile widens. Then his pants are off and he's standing naked, and my breath stutters in my throat.

He's magnificent. Of course, I knew that. But seeing him like this, all sculpted planes and gleaming skin, the need to have my lips on him is so intense, I rise from the bed, reaching for him.

Only to stop, when he shakes his head.

Reaching down, he gently presses me back onto the bed.

"Not yet," he says, before taking the edge of my shirt and pulling it up and over me.

His eyes survey my face, caressing my throat, my breasts. He's breathing hard, the rise and fall of his chest mirroring mine.

My eyes slide down his muscular thighs, and I swallow down the lust running through me. He leans down, takes my hand, and presses it to his arousal. I grip him without even realizing it, massaging him, and he groans aloud.

Desire burns my lower belly and the sound of it seems to arouse him even more, for he hardens further, throbbing under my palm.

"You're in my blood," he says, his voice hoarse.

Before I can react, he bends down and kisses me right between my thighs and the heat in my belly explodes. I cry out, and he pulls my jeans down my legs, taking my panties with it. He flings them off, before taking his mouth back to me. The touch of his lips on the most intimate part of me sends spasms of desire through me. And when he thrusts his tongue inside, I can't hold back anymore. The violet spark in my heart bursts to life. It zooms up my spine, up my neck, blinding me before exploding into flames above me.

I hear a low keening cry and know it's me. I can't believe it is possible to even feel such scorching heat. Dissolving every barrier inside. And before the spasms even stop, he's inside me.

He thrusts into me, going right inside even as I half-rise off the bed, writhing with the jolts of desire that pound through me.

Then I am rising for real, for he's pulled me up by my arms, winding them around his neck. My legs coil around his waist.

He curls my hair around his palm, pulling at it, sending another sharp jolt of heat through me.

"Open your eyes, Leana. Look at me," he commands.

And when my eyes fly open, it is to be captured by the sliver green of his. He moves slightly inside me, pulsing liquid passion through me, and I gasp aloud. He's filling me, pulling at me to give in. He wants to mark me inside, make sure there is only him.

Only him.

"You're mine," he says, thrusting into me. "Mine."

I can't reply. The intensity of him is overwhelming.

The colors flowing off him are a stream of gold and green, wrapping around me, pulling me to him, binding me to him with every thrust. All I can do is hold onto him, as he slams into me, this time going so deep, deeper still, that I cry out. My body arches back as wave after wave of pleasure sweeps through me, pushing me out of my body, so I almost black out when I come.

His hoarse cry mingles with mine as he pours himself into me.

When I come back into my body, it is to find I am on my back, my heart still racing, or maybe it's his heartbeat I hear. He lies on top of me, our legs entwined, his shoulders pushing me into the bed.

When I move, he raises himself on his forearms. His biceps glisten with sweat, muscles bunching as he supports himself, so his weight is partially off me.

"Yours," I tell him, my voice soft, lips curving slightly, matching his as he smiles.

I feel curiously light. That weight holding me down dissolves. And when I look inside, I find my wolf, ready to shift.

Micah senses it too, senses my animal.

He slides off me and stands up, holding out his hand.

When I take it, he pulls my sweat-glistening body to my feet.

"Go, Leana," he says. "Run free."

Darting a grateful look at him, I take a step forward, then another, before relaxing into my wolf. I let my body elongate, shimmer, flow into my animal self.

Letting the world shift into sharper, deeper focus, I see through my wolf's eyes.

Going to the balcony, he flings it open, and I follow him onto the deck. Beyond us, the garden slopes down to the beach.

The stars lighting up the night sky reflect off the white of the waves.

Stepping onto the grass, I stretch out, shake myself, let my muscles grow into my true form.

Turning over my shoulder, I tilt my head. *Are you with me?*

Always, he replies.

EPILOGUE

A few days later

SOMETHING SHIFTS IN THE DEPTHS of the Arabian Sea. Something dark and soulless. A shadow. A stain on the sea floor, with a core so bleak it seems to fade into nothing. And at its center, a dot. A pinprick of red that pulses, glowing in the pale sunlight flickering down through the layers of the deep sea.

As weeks go by, the red increases in size, bleeding out into the blackness, encircling it. The shadow takes shape, drawing life from the plankton around it. It draws from the life essence of plants and passing shoals of fish. As it grows in size, it preys on the larger fish and sea creatures.

The red pulses brighter, as the black takes on the shape of a male. Until it ascends to the surface. The sea currents push it out. Push it toward land, toward shore.

Reaching the beach, the black creeps through the sand, unwatched by anyone but a stray dog that senses the evil within it and retreats. As it bleeds up the brown sand, up toward the path leading up to the city, it leaves no trace behind.

The darkness had underestimated the light, but this time it would bide its time.

The End

✧ ✧ ✧

Continue the Many Lives Series here
amazon.com/author/laxmihariharan

✦ ✦ ✦

Newsletter
http://smarturl.it/Laxmi

ABOUT THE AUTHOR

Laxmi Hariharan is a New York Times bestselling author. Married to a filmmaker and fellow author she lives in London.

Follow her on twitter @laxmi